F DRUCKER
35250000972455
89af
Drucker, Eugene, 1952-
The savior : a novel

7/07

P9-BZI-517

8/7/07
OCT 1 2 2007
11/29/07
Dec
07

THE SAVIOR

A NOVEL

Eugene Drucker

SIMON & SCHUSTER
NEW YORK LONDON TORONTO SYDNEY

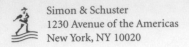

Simon & Schuster
1230 Avenue of the Americas
New York, NY 10020

This book is a work of fiction. Names, characters, places, and incidents either are products of the author's imagination or are used fictitiously. Any resemblance to actual events or locales or persons, living or dead, is entirely coincidental.

Copyright © 2007 by Eugene Drucker

All rights reserved, including the right to reproduce this book or portions thereof in any form whatsoever. For information address Simon & Schuster Subsidiary Rights Department, 1230 Avenue of the Americas, New York, NY 10020

First Simon & Schuster hardcover edition July 2007

SIMON & SCHUSTER and colophon are registered trademarks of Simon & Schuster, Inc.

"Threadsuns" from *Selected Poems and Prose by Paul Celan*, translated by John Felstiner. Copyright © 2001 by John Felstiner. Used by permission of W.W. Norton & Company, Inc.

For information about special discounts for bulk purchases, please contact Simon & Schuster Special Sales at 1-800-456-6798 or business@simonandschuster.com.

Designed by Davina Mock-Maniscalco

Manufactured in the United States of America

10 9 8 7 6 5 4 3 2 1

Library of Congress Cataloging-in-Publication Data

Drucker, Eugene, date.
  The savior : a novel / Eugene Drucker.
    p. cm.
  1. Violinists—Fiction. 2. Concentration camps—Fiction. 3. Concentration camp inmates—Fiction. 4. World War, 1939–1945—Fiction. I. Title.

PS3604.R83S38 2007
813'.6—dc22

                          2007000999

ISBN-13: 978-1-4165-4329-9
ISBN-10:   1-4165-4329-5

To Roberta, who has shared a long journey with me;
to Julian, our delight;
and in memory of my father, Ernest Drucker

How sour sweet music is
When time is broke and no proportion kept!
So is it in the music of men's lives.

—Shakespeare, *Richard II,*
act 5, scene 5

GESTAPO OFFICER [gesturing toward *Guernica*]: Did you do this?
PICASSO: No, you did.

THE SAVIOR

I

I used to play for the wounded and dying. The Army sent me; it was supposed to help the war effort.

"Can you play *Wiener Blut*?"

He shook his head.

"How about 'Es war ein Edelweiss, ein kleines Edelweiss'?" asked the one with the wooden leg.

Before Gottfried Keller could answer, someone behind him shouted, "'Das Horst Wessel Lied'!" Keller turned just in time to see a baldheaded soldier propelling his wheelchair furiously toward the center of the room with a few swift thrusts of his powerful arms. The soldier spun around to face the violinist, who noticed a jagged line of stitch marks on the man's scalp. Keller had already explained that he couldn't play tunes on request, that he'd prepared a whole program of solo violin music.

The air was stuffy in the abandoned schoolhouse. Judging from the look of things, it had been converted into a hospital only within the last couple of weeks. An outdated map of German conquests, from 1942 or the first half of '43, hung lop-sided above a blackboard; desks and chairs were stacked against the wall. The bedridden were arranged along two of the other walls, on either side of him, and in the middle of the room several rows of men fidgeted in their wheelchairs. A few bulbs hanging from the ceiling cast a yellowish light onto their faces. The floors had been mopped with so much ammonia that his nostrils were stinging, but there was another smell in the room that even the ammonia couldn't block out—the sweet-tinged reek of all those feverish, sweaty bodies packed together in too small a space.

The windows were latched shut. Winter was coming.

Sneers, grimaces—they didn't care what he had prepared. It didn't help when he told them that the music he wanted to play was more challenging than the tunes they were demand-ing, which all needed piano accompaniment and would sound incomplete without it, while his music was complete just as he was going to play it. Eyes all around him, peering out from bandaged faces, near-extinguished eyes boring holes in him, all asking the same question: why had he come to bother them with this crap?

He began to play Bach, and the man with the shaven head swung his wheelchair around so that he was facing the wall.

Idiots, he said to himself. He was there to help, to make life a bit less unpleasant for them, to make their recovery easier. And for those who would never recover? Well, to lend some dignity, some meaning to their final days. At least that was the official line, mouthed again and again by the men behind desks who sent him on these fruitless missions.

Keller had barely finished the first phrase when the sol-diers started talking—to one another, or to him, he didn't know which, he was trying so hard to shut out the sounds of their voices. Then whistling, even singing out of tune, pretending to sing along with the melodies he was playing. Making fun of Bach: no matter how tone-deaf they were, he couldn't believe they would sing so badly if they were really trying to trace the shape of the music with their voices.

They weren't singing with him. They were singing against him: he had become the enemy.

━━━━━━━━━━

"Why aren't you in uniform, Herr Geiger?" asked the ringleader in another ward. There was a stump where his right arm should have been.

He hadn't bothered to learn Keller's name. None of the patients took the trouble to remember it, even when a doctor introduced him before he played. If any of them ever addressed him, it was always as "Fiddler," sometimes with "Herr" before it in a show of mock respect.

"I'm not in the Army."

"Yes, of course, that's obvious. But why not?"

"Yeah," chimed in two or three others. "Why not?"

"A weak heart," Keller replied, barely moving his lips. The soldier cupped his hand behind his left ear and leaned forward, inching closer with his wheelchair. Keller cleared his throat and said again, "A weak heart. I didn't pass the physical."

"Oh, a weak heart," the invalid repeated in a mock-sympathetic tone, staring thoughtfully at Keller's chest. "I see. You mean . . . you're a weakling."

"A weakling!" echoed the chorus of his followers.

"How touching," added the ringleader, the pain in his face transformed to triumph.

"Well, he's in better shape than we are now," said someone sitting up in a bed in the corner of the room.

The one-armed soldier turned and glared at him.

"Be quiet already!" The bedridden soldier, who seemed to be forcing his voice to rise above a whisper, was in worse shape than the others. His midriff was covered with reddened bandages. His forehead was beaded with sweat, and his eyes were so sunken that Keller couldn't tell whom the man was looking at when he spoke. Or perhaps he was looking at nobody, just staring at the wall. "Let him play," he said wearily. "It's our only break from this damned routine."

"This is worse!" jeered another patient. There was laughter all around, but Keller ignored their mockery. By now he was used to it. He kept looking at the man in the corner; something about the thin frame propped up against those pillows grabbed at his heart. The soldier was biting his lower lip, squinting as if the meager light in there was too much for him.

Clutching his instrument, Keller wondered what the man meant about the routine. Injections? Bedpans? False encouragement when there wasn't much hope? Or was it that they all had to be crammed together every hour of the day? Isolated from the others, this man seemed to have nothing left to buoy his spirits—no defiance, no swagger, no ability to laugh at another's weakness.

That's how I would look.

"I'll die of boredom if I don't die of this first," rasped Keller's defender, pointing to his belly. Every word he spoke sounded as if it had been pushed through a wall of pain. "Come on, let him play! It might do us all some good."

The effort of raising his voice brought on a coughing fit, and he fell back in his bed. The others had stopped laughing. When the coughing subsided, Keller began to play, wishing he could speak to that man, reach out to him in his loneliness. But after the performance he had to leave right away. His driver was waiting; there were two other hospitals on the schedule for that day. Out in the corridor, he looked back toward the room from which he'd just emerged, thinking to go back in after some of the other patients—the ones who could move on their own—had come out. But then he glanced at his wristwatch. It was already half past eleven: there was no time left.

———————————

A few weeks later he was driven three hours west to a small town near the front. He tried to stay calm, as always during these rides, but he never knew exactly where he was being taken. He could only hope they wouldn't get too close to any fighting. From experience, he knew better than to attempt a meaningful conversation with the driver—about music, the wounded soldiers, or the war.

The driver had told him when they started that it would be a long ride. After a while he closed his eyes and tried to doze off, since he hadn't slept well the night before. He wasn't sure he could relax enough to take a nap, but they had smooth roads that day, and he found the steady motion of the car rather soothing. His thoughts wandered back to his days at the Hochschule—the friends he'd had there, the confidence he used to feel as a player—and then, despite his efforts to think of something else, to Marietta.

He pictured a small figure hunched over the keyboard in a practice studio, the pale oval of a face turned and uplifted in anticipation of his cue to start the next phrase. He could still feel his arm around her waist, pulling her toward him as they walked through the streets of Cologne that winter, before everything changed. So much time had passed that he couldn't clearly see her. He hardly ever looked anymore at the snapshots he'd taken during one of their strolls along the Rhine embankments. She was bundled up in an overcoat and her face was partly hidden by a scarf. The pictures were faded after all these years, their contrasts ill defined, the lines blurred.

He must have fallen asleep after all; when he opened his eyes, they were winding their way through the cobbled streets of a small town, close to their destination. Keller was relieved to see that all the buildings were intact—so far, the village had been spared. But the driver told him that the roads and bridges not far to the west and north had been bombed and the flow of supplies choked off. The streets were eerily quiet and empty except for a cluster of hollow-cheeked children, unkempt, dirty, their clothes tattered, pawing through the contents of an overturned garbage can.

Where he lived, things weren't quite so bad, at least not yet. Still, it was months since he'd had a decent cut of meat, and he could barely remember the smell or taste of fresh vegetables. He could only imagine the way they had *looked* many years before, on display every weekend in the Marktplatz of the small town in Westphalia where he grew up. But recently he'd begun to think about chocolate more than any other food, trying to remember how it felt as he bit off a piece, trying to imagine its stickiness, the rush of pleasure that always used to come with the first few bites as his tongue crushed the bar against the roof of his mouth. He dreamed about chocolate. Sometimes it took an effort to convince himself that the Wehrmacht wasn't going to reward him for his performances one of these days with a box of sweets or a bottle of cognac.

A civilian hospital at the western edge of that town near the front had been taken over by the Army as it retreated eastward. The hospital was a low, blocklike structure of pale brick, bordered on one side by wooded parkland and on the other by a cemetery whose marble headstones glistened in the sun. On the road flanking the graveyard an ambulance sped past Keller's car, its siren wailing. It pulled up next to the emergency entrance. Two medics jumped out, threw open the back doors and unloaded a cargo of four or five wounded soldiers. An arm dangled from one of the stretchers, which tipped perilously from side to side as it was taken out.

Because of the sudden arrival of the new patients, Keller had to wait over an hour before he could start to play. Sitting in the corridor while his driver went out to smoke, he tried to run through some music in his head. A man approached his chair with small, shuffling steps, mumbling to himself. He looked as if he were wearing a mask: there were bandages all over his face and the top of his head, tied in double and triple thicknesses, with small holes for the mouth, nostrils and eyes. To Keller's relief, the man shuffled past as if nobody else was there.

All he wanted was to take out his violin, get it over with and go home. But little was waiting for him there—meager rations in the cupboard, an empty bed.

His friends were all gone: drafted, sent to the Russian front. Except the few who had fled years earlier, while there was still time—that is, the ones who'd had sense. And the ones who'd had no choice.

His parents had died within six months of each other, soon after the war began. He hadn't been very close to them for years. They knew little about music and didn't understand much about his hopes for a concertmaster position or a solo career. They had married late; he was their only child. There were some cousins, but he'd lost touch with them. It was just as well: they wouldn't have agreed on what was happening all around them.

A doctor eventually came over to greet him. The man in the mask, still wandering in the hallway, passed within a few inches of them.

"A severe head wound?" Keller asked once the man was out of earshot.

"Yes and no," the doctor replied, smoothing back a strand of copper-colored hair that had strayed over his forehead.

"I'm afraid I don't understand."

For a few seconds the doctor seemed not to have heard him. There were dark circles under his bloodshot eyes. Keller wondered when he'd last had a full night's sleep. With both fronts caving in, there were plenty of casualties these days: he probably had to perform emergency surgery at all hours of the day and night, whenever new patients were rushed in. Between two fingers he held the stub of a cigarette, still lit. His cuticles were bloody and scabby; he seemed to make a habit of chewing at them.

Finally he cleared his throat and explained: "There has been no physical wound to the head. He put those bandages on himself, and insists on keeping them. He doesn't give us much trouble, though—he's in his own world."

"Well, maybe he's better off than the rest of us," said Keller on an impulse.

The doctor looked at him quizzically for a few seconds. Keller was surprised at himself, surprised that he'd ventured to say something like that to a stranger, but the doctor struck him as a man who knew how things stood. He knew they were losing—that was obvious from one look at his tired, hopeless face.

The patient disappeared through a doorway, and the doctor tipped his head back, as if to indicate the same door by pointing with his chin. "That's the room where you're supposed to play." He looked back at the violinist, his brow creased, as though he doubted the performance could do any good. "I hope you can achieve some results with them."

Keller approached the door, wondering what distractions, what insults were awaiting him.

Most of the patients in the room were bedridden, attached to intravenous tubes suspended from metal poles standing between their beds. Late afternoon sunlight was pouring through a narrow casement window directly opposite the door. The other windows were shuttered, as though the patients had just awakened from a nap, and much of the room was in shadow. Dust motes floated in the shaft of light. Sitting in a chair that he had pulled into the light just as Keller entered, the man in the mask watched his every move as he took the violin out of its case and tightened the hair of the bow.

"Have you come to heal us?" he asked.

Some of the other patients snickered, but Keller didn't know whether the question was meant to be sarcastic. It was impossible to tell, since there was barely room for the man to move his jaw, and the words came out low and muffled from behind all those layers of bandage.

"Can you make us whole again?"

Keller wasn't sure how to answer him. He wondered what the authorities would expect him to say in a situation like this. But he knew he had to find his own words, had to respond as truthfully as possible without sounding hopeless.

"Music has been known to have a therapeutic effect," he said after a long hesitation. "That's why I'm here. I'm going to play the Chaconne by Bach for you. There is great power in this music—a spiritual power that . . ."

"But is there *magical* power in it?" asked the mask.

"Magical?" Keller repeated.

"You know what I mean. Can it bring back the dead?"

II

A week had passed since the last performance. It was very early in the morning, and he was still groggy from yet another night of uneasy sleep; he had dreamt about the man in the mask, who was pestering him with questions he could barely hear. The man's words became less and less intelligible as Keller approached him, and he tottered, arms outstretched, then fell backward before Keller could grab his hand.

He had no appetite for breakfast, but gulped down some coffee before he picked up the violin and headed out the door of his apartment. On the way downstairs, just before he reached the ground floor, he noticed that the sidewalk in front of the building was lit up.

Headlights.

A car? Here, at this hour?

He heard the hum of an engine idling; then, as the inner door shut behind him, he peered through the glass panel in the door to the street.

It was an open car, like the jeeps used by the Wehrmacht to take him to the makeshift hospitals near the front. But they never came to his house. He always picked up his assignments at Headquarters and was sent out directly from there; with the condition of most of the roads these days, there was no time to lose circling back through the one-way streets of the town.

The driver cocked his head when he saw him hesitating in the doorway, and gestured with his thumb toward the back seat. It was too late for Keller to pretend he hadn't noticed him, too late to withdraw into the shadows of the stairwell. Reluctantly, he pushed open the door.

"Get in."

The driver was square-jawed, solidly built. His overcoat was unbuttoned, despite the intense cold, and in the pale light from a nearby street lamp, Keller could see the crisp black uniform: SS, not Wehrmacht.

He stepped gingerly around an ice-rimmed puddle, holding the violin case against his body, cradling it with both arms. "I was on my way to Headquarters, to pick up my next assignment."

"I just came from there. They sent me to fetch you."

My diary. Have they gotten their hands on it?

Or could he thank Herr Maier for this?

He looked up and down the street, wondering if anyone was watching. A scrawny gray cat darted across the cobblestones. Before disappearing into an alleyway opposite his house, it locked eyes with him for a moment.

The storefronts were dark, and all the windows shuttered, as if the winding row of narrow, gabled houses had retreated into itself in an effort to shut out the winter chill. It seemed to Keller that the entire street had closed its eyes to the disappearance of a neighbor.

The driver was staring at him, tapping the gloved fingers of his right hand on the steering wheel. Keller tried to clear his head and think decisively. If this was just another variation on the theme of his pointless performances for the soldiers—if everything was still all right—then any attempt to argue his way out would only make the driver suspicious. It was probably a mistake even to hesitate.

"May I ask where we are going?"

The driver handed him a dispatch from Headquarters as he settled himself in the back of the car, carefully placing his instrument on the seat next to him. He pulled off his gloves. It took some effort to keep his hands steady as he opened the envelope. Inside was a typewritten sheet embossed with the Wehrmacht letterhead. He read the message several times, trying to understand what was happening.

Your services are required by the SS for the next four
days. Normal activities to resume this weekend.

There were no details, no explanations. He recognized the signature of the lieutenant who usually authorized his transport.

He looked up at the driver. "Are you taking me . . . to a camp?"

The driver turned to face him, his lips curling into a smile. "Our Kommandant is a great music-lover."

It must be the one by the chemical factory, near the bend in the river. A place he had always avoided thinking about. It was fifteen kilometers from the town, off the main road, so he had never been driven very close to it on his trips to play for the soldiers. But he'd heard about that camp from time to time. There was a village not far away, and people talked. Someone had seen a long line of emaciated prisoners leaving the factory one night. No one he knew, though, had heard much about the camp itself.

"If I'm supposed to be there for the next four days, I'll need to bring some things along. Unless you're planning to drive me back and forth each day."

"All your needs will be taken care of. You'll be quite comfortable there." The driver looked at Keller's right hand, which was gripping the door handle, as if he was daring him to pull on it. Keller let go of the handle, leaned back and put his gloves on again.

He had no idea why they were sending him there, but if he were being arrested, the driver probably wouldn't have come by himself. There would have been a couple of armed guards to make sure he couldn't get away. This thought, rational as it was, didn't set his mind at ease, and he was seized with longing for the drab familiarity of his home—the old overstuffed armchair in which he often fell asleep while reading or studying scores late at night, the large bay windows through which he'd stare at the rooftops across the street while he practiced, even the cramped, poorly equipped kitchen alcove where he would open ration tins and attempt to cook something palatable. He looked back at the house as the car pulled away from the curb, trying not to be too obvious while gazing up at those fourth-floor windows.

As they turned into the next street, he noticed that his left hand was stroking the violin case. He stopped himself as he saw the driver looking at him through the rearview mirror. For a few moments he couldn't decide what to do with his hands. Finally he folded them in his lap.

It had rained during the night, and then the rain had turned to sleet and hail, which had ricocheted off the skylight in his bedroom while he tried to sleep. By daybreak the sky was clearing: as they drove past a few clusters of dreary little houses on the outskirts of town, the mist overhead thinned out, a shroud of gray yielding to pale blue fringed with pink near the horizon. But the weak winter sun gave off little warmth. Keller pulled up his coat collar and tightened his scarf; he could feel his shoulders hunching up. His eyes were watering, and his cheeks stung when the wind slapped his face.

Stretches of the road were icy. Though the driver navigated around the ruts and snowdrifts skillfully enough, Keller started to feel nauseous from all the swerving and bouncing. Suddenly the car lurched, then rocked backward. With his left hand he grabbed for the violin and managed to hold it in its place, but he was thrown against the front seat.

"Scheisse," muttered the driver, opening his door and looking back at the left rear wheel, which was stuck in a thick bed of mud. "We'll have to get out and push."

Glad for the delay and for the respite from that ride, Keller clambered out of the car. His chest hurt where it had slammed into the front seat. He rubbed the sore spot gingerly, glancing up and down the road. There was no traffic moving in either direction. Next to them was a huge field covered with ice, dotted here and there with gnarled trees whose branches groped toward the sky.

Like misshapen fingers, he thought. If he'd been wandering out there alone, he would have found a bleak, desolate beauty in the landscape.

With the driver at his side, he strained at first to force the car out of its rut, throwing all his weight against the back fender. But after a few minutes he stopped concentrating on what they were doing, felt his arms slacken. He stared into the field, trying to imagine what torments were in store for him today, lowering his head beneath his shoulders whenever there was a gust of wind.

The huge fellow next to him was having no trouble, or at

least didn't want to show it. No gasps of effort from him. He kept readjusting his grip on the fender, planting his feet further and further apart. Occasionally he lunged and stabbed at the icy mud with a shovel, then ran up to the driver's seat and pumped the accelerator, but the engine shrilled and the wheels spun in place while Keller breathed in a blast of exhaust. After several futile attempts at the steering wheel, the driver stayed at Keller's side, pushing, backing away a few steps and ramming the fender with all his might. The jeep rocked back and forth. Their heads were so close together that the condensation from their breath mingled into one gray cloud of mist, constantly renewed, contrasting with the brutal clarity of the thin, dry air. Finally, after he had kicked and shoveled the sludge away from both rear wheels, the driver managed to free the car from its muddy prison.

"It's about time," he said. "Now I'll have to step on it. The Kommandant doesn't like to be kept waiting."

Keller hadn't dressed warmly enough. Climbing into the back seat again, he began to shiver. He picked up his violin case and clutched it to his chest, as if that could keep out the cold.

Ever since he'd started playing for the Wehrmacht, he thought he had nothing to worry about. But why were they sending him *there*? So far he had played only for soldiers, never for prisoners. His performances were supposed to soothe and comfort people. He almost always failed in the attempt, of course. But that was the idea, anyway: a humane gesture.

He didn't know exactly who was being held at that camp— Jews, he supposed, or Russian prisoners of war. Or Germany's homegrown Communists, if there were any left. Yet one thing was clear to him: toward prisoners there would be no humane gestures.

"Excuse me, but could you tell me something about this camp? Until now I've played only in hospitals."

He could see the driver eyeing him through the rearview mirror. "There isn't much to say about it. You'll see it soon enough."

"If I'm supposed to play, it would help me to get some idea of . . . of my listeners, so I can plan a program."

The driver slowed down, turned around—though the car was still moving—and gave Keller a long look. His cold gray eyes pinned the violinist to the back of his seat.

Maybe they . . . But he hadn't said or done anything that would attract attention. He always did as he was told. What more did they want from him?

Had he misjudged that doctor last week? But who could argue with what he had said about the man who'd swathed himself in all those bandages? It was a simple fact: these days madmen were better off than anyone who had to look reality in the face.

There was his diary, yes. He always kept it in a locked drawer of his desk, knowing that the lock could be pried open if someone was really looking for something. But he'd never thought he was important enough for that kind of scrutiny.

He had written with disgust about the hospital concerts, but more often than not it was disgust with himself, with his level of playing. In one entry he had questioned the point of playing for soldiers who were apathetic or hostile. He remembered now that he had called it a meaningless exercise. But could that be held against him? Was it enough to send him on this ride?

He'd been careful not to write anything disrespectful about the officers and doctors he met. Once he had even taken the precaution of making an entry full of praise for the Wehrmacht and the SS. Afterward, whenever he leafed through the diary and glanced at that page, he laughed. But then he would shudder slightly: the insincerity might be as obvious to prying eyes as it was to his own. They weren't fools, and the more he thought about it now, on the way to the camp, the more his exaggerations of their heroism seemed laced with sarcasm. He wished he had torn the page out.

Trying to calm down, Keller reminded himself that there had never been any signs of tampering in his apartment. Everything was always as he had left it, thank God. So if it wasn't the diary, then . . . Ernst, or Marietta. A Jewish friend and a Jewish girlfriend. But he'd known both of them years earlier, before the Nuremberg laws were passed. He'd had no contact with either one since 1935. Surely the authorities had more important matters to deal with.

Had someone in the building been spying on him?

Herr Maier, his downstairs neighbor, might have heard the music he sometimes practiced when he couldn't get past his problems in Bach and Paganini. The jagged edges of Hindemith, Bartók and Berg soothed him, allowing him to bypass his usual frustrations on the instrument. He felt like he was really getting something done, because there were new, clear-cut challenges to deal with—passages to learn, fingerings and bowings to work out. There was also a kind of titillation, a furtive thrill as he closed all the windows and doors in his apartment, put on a heavy practice mute and tackled "degenerate" music that had been banned from the concert stage. He did it only after all his neighbors had left for work, but the previous week he'd heard that Herr Maier, who lived directly below his apartment, was laid up for a couple of days with the flu. He had almost finished learning a Romanian Rhapsody by Bartók, and simply couldn't wait for Maier's fever to go down before he got his hands on those wonderful quirky patterns and once again felt the bounce of those lopsided rhythms. Folk music of the Untermenschen, from the lands they'd conquered in the East.

But he doubted that jowly, thick-featured Maier, who worked in some sort of factory on the fringes of town, would be able to tell the difference between Bartók and Beethoven. So, if he was tone-deaf, and if Ernst and Marietta were too long ago to matter, what was there to worry about?

Keller thought of the atonal piece he'd dared to write for solo violin. Though it had no roots in the folk music of the East, it would have been branded as degenerate just the same. But he'd never tried to get it published, and for the past few months he hadn't practiced a note of it; the manuscript was always locked in the same drawer as his diary.

He got along well enough with most of his neighbors, yet there was no love lost between him and Herr Maier. Could Maier be the one, after all? Even if he didn't know what Keller was practicing? He tended to look at the violinist suspiciously whenever they met at the front door or on the landing outside his apartment. He would screw up his beady eyes as he glanced at the violin case, and hardly responded to Keller's observations about the weather as he turned his fleshy back to him and put his key in the door. Of course, Keller knew better than to talk to him even casually about the latest war news. He assumed Maier was wondering why he wasn't off at the front, fighting for the Fatherland. The older man seemed to view the violin as the embodiment of a bohemian lifestyle that was alien to his notions of order. But Keller knew there was no way to be sure of what was going through his mind, and usually had no trouble forgetting about him when their paths didn't cross.

The car went into a skid and he was jolted from his thoughts. The driver managed to regain control without slowing down. After they rounded a curve in the road, Keller could make out a cluster of squat buildings in the distance. At first their outlines were indistinct, as if veiled in mist—a strange sight on that cold, clear day. When they got a bit closer, he noticed one larger structure with several chimneys belching dark smoke. There was an acrid odor that intensified as they approached.

He had passed through industrial zones before and during the war, had smelled his share of noxious fumes. Recently, on the way to a hospital performance, he had been driven past a munitions plant struck only a few hours earlier by Allied bombs. Flames were still smoldering in every part of the ruined complex; plumes of black and gray smoke billowed up into the sky. The driver and Keller had both had to cover their faces with handkerchiefs as they crawled through the haze.

But here—this smell, this smoke—there were no signs of disruption, no ambulances or fire engines racing toward the camp. The SS driver proceeded at a normal speed and didn't even seem to notice what Keller was staring at. This smoke was not the result of a bombing. It appeared to be part of everyday life, probably the by-product of some new chemical process.

This time he couldn't find a handkerchief in his pocket. He cupped a hand tightly around his nose and mouth, and closed his eyes until the sting subsided. The eruptions from the chimneys stopped after a few minutes, but the smoke hovered over the camp a while longer, an opaque cloud that gradually thinned into streaks and wisps of gray floating upward into the blueness of the sky.

The final approach ran parallel to some railroad tracks on the right, which seemed to end at a platform surrounded by a cluster of warehouses. On the left, through a double fence of barbed wire, he could see row after row of identical barracks. They looked as if they had been thrown together in a hurry with cheap wooden planks, providing the barest minimum of shelter. In the middle of the camp there was a large empty space, almost the size of an athletic field.

They drove alongside the fence for several minutes before they reached a massive iron gate with a watchtower looming above. The driver identified himself, and two sentries opened the gate. As they drove in, Keller noticed a broad ditch between the fences, which stretched to the left and right as far as he could see.

III

The antique bookcase seemed out of place, didn't fit in with the purely functional desk and chairs. Behind its wood-latticed glass doors a set of leather-bound books occupied three shelves: the collected works of Goethe, whose name was engraved on the spine of each with gold letters. On other shelves stood less ornate but equally massive volumes.

"Why do you think you are here?"

The question caught him off guard. "I had assumed you'd like me to play."

The Kommandant nodded, waiting for more. He was tall, lean, probably in his early fifties, with steel-gray hair brushed back rather severely from his high forehead. He was wearing the black uniform of the Allgemeine SS. The silver oak leaf on each side of his collar showed his rank: Standartenführer.

"For the inmates . . ." Keller ventured, half question, half answer. Then, after a few more seconds: "I have to admit I was asking myself the same thing."

"So why didn't you ask me directly? As soon as you came in?"

"I didn't think it was my place, Herr Kommandant. I never question orders."

A smile flashed across the Kommandant's face as he leaned forward, folding his hands on top of the desk. He wasn't as stiff as most of the officers Keller had met. His manner seemed relaxed, almost casual. "Technically that's correct, since you're working for the Wehrmacht. But as an artist, you can hardly be expected to do your best if you're simply following orders."

Keller had been ready to receive instructions, orders, to be shuttled back and forth like a pawn to do their bidding, but he hadn't expected anyone to tell him how he should think and feel *as an artist.*

"And I will need for you to do your best," he continued. "You see, you've been asked to come here for the final stage of an experiment. But before I tell you about it, let me ask you another question. The audience you're going to play for—the inmates here—what do you know about them? Who do you think they are?"

Better not to seem to know too much.

"Jews?" Keller offered, after a few moments' hesitation. That much was safe. After all, how could anyone fail to notice that all the Jews had disappeared?

The Kommandant's brow furrowed slightly as his eyes probed Keller's.

"I haven't heard much about this place, sir. I mean, I knew there was a . . . a labor camp not far from the city, but I didn't know where it was, or how it was run. Or exactly who was here."

The Kommandant let out a little sigh. "You should understand at least this much about the whole system of camps, here and in the East: the aim is to separate Jews and other Untermenschen, like Gypsies, from our pure German stock, to end the racial and moral contamination that has corrupted us for centuries."

His eyes had taken on a slightly glazed look, as if he wasn't listening to his own words because he had said and heard the same thing too many times. Was he testing him? Keller was careful not to react; only polite attention could be read in his face. He wondered, though, just how much of an act he would have to put on. Did he have to show how zealous he could be, performing the tasks the Kommandant was going to set?

"It's true that we need the labor provided by the camp populations. At the factory nearby, we help manufacture shells and spare parts for tanks. Within the camp itself, we've set up a plant where rubber is synthesized through a special new process. You probably noticed the smoke as you drove up. Yes, that's the only drawback—the smell. It gets in your clothes, your hair, even flavors the food you eat." He smiled and shook his head slightly. "The price one has to pay for progress."

Through the window of the office, beyond several rows of wooden barracks, Keller could make out the long, flat-roofed building with the chimneys. It was made of stone and had no windows, at least none that he could see.

"By the way, don't expect to see a normal workforce—conditions here are pretty rough. We take as many sanitary precautions as possible, so there haven't been any outbreaks of typhus. But rations are extremely low. You're going to see a lot of very thin people in a state of exhaustion. Don't let it distract you when you perform."

Keller was grateful that neither Ernst nor Marietta had ended up in a place like this. But he wondered what had happened to the other Jews he'd known: stand partners in various orchestras he had worked in, a couple of theory and music history professors during his first two years at the Hochschule.

Good people, as German as the rest of us, he thought. Could any of them be here? And the Jewish children he'd seen in the years just before the war started, even during the first few months of the war—neighbors' kids in the stairwells of buildings where he had lived, solemn-faced youngsters on their way to school, the yellow star sewn onto their jackets. What had become of all the children?

"Cigarette?"

"No thank you, Herr Kommandant."

He reached into the desk drawer and took out a silver cigarette case, watching Keller all the while. With precise movements his long, bony fingers found the clasp, opened the cover and drew a cigarette to his lips. From a jacket pocket he brought out a gold lighter, and took his time lighting up.

"The scientific possibilities offered by camps like this are what interest me the most." He inhaled deeply, his gaze drifting toward the window. Then he looked back at his guest and added quickly, sotto voce through a haze of smoke, "Imagine how outmoded animal experimentation seems now."

A shadow of disgust passed across Keller's face; a moment of satisfaction was evident in the Kommandant's. The thin mouth puckered slightly, tugging upward at the corners. Behind the wire-rimmed glasses, his gray eyes narrowed like those of a purring cat.

"The authorities have recruited people from the medical and scientific communities to conduct research in some of the camps. I had the good fortune to be chosen for this sort of work."

There seemed to be a touch of pride in this statement, as if he was anxious to distinguish himself from the soldiers and officers Keller had been spending most of his time with recently. Keller tried to look impressed.

"This camp is relatively small," added the Kommandant. "Of course, there are quotas to fill, production demands to be met, but the inspectors from Oranienburg don't get here too often. So I can be flexible and pursue my interests."

He got up, walked across the room and back, then sat down on the corner of the mahogany desk. Supporting his weight with one hand, his legs extended to a spot on the floor a few feet away, he took a long, voluptuous drag on his cigarette.

"By its very nature, a camp like this is an experiment in endurance. Try to imagine it. When you're crowded together with so many others, everything changes in your outlook. There's no privacy. Personal possessions take on an entirely different meaning: what few things you manage to hold on to—a cup, a spoon—may become your sole means of making it from one day to the next. You're hungry all the time, you have to work past the point of exhaustion, and the guards . . . well, we can't control them every instant, you know."

Keller didn't want to imagine the living conditions or the people the Kommandant was describing. All he wanted was to go home. A few hours earlier he'd been lying in bed, listening to the raindrops beating against the skylight. It took an effort to keep his eyes from welling up at the thought.

Why can't he just tell me what he needs me to do? Then I could figure out how to do it and get out of here.

"All these factors sap not only one's strength but also the will to survive. That's what I've been studying for the past three years, that's what fascinates me in these people—the survival instinct, with all its different strategies and variations in strength. Winners and losers are sorted out pretty quickly here."

He smiled, looked out the window for a few moments,

then fastened his eyes on Keller again. "The camp is a de facto human laboratory, constantly demonstrating Darwin's great theory. You know the one I mean, don't you? The survival of the fittest, or in this case, of those who adapt the best to a radically changed environment."

There was a sink in one corner, its white porcelain immaculate and gleaming. Staring at it, Keller imagined splotches of red on the rim, in the basin, on the wall behind it. Suddenly he could see the faucet being turned on by bloody hands, the stains disappearing in a whirlpool of brownish liquid.

"Have there been many deaths, Herr Kommandant?" The answer was obvious from what he had already been told, but he felt obligated to respond once in a while.

"Unfortunately." The Kommandant's face assumed a mournful expression, in contrast to the animation with which he spoke. "Conditions here are so abnormal, so . . . beyond the pale of what we think of as human life in society, that even those who are surviving can't be described as truly alive. The question is, can they ever be brought back to life from this living death?"

It was strange that he was referring to the Jews and whoever else was here with terms like *human* and *society* instead of the usual vilifications.

Keller remembered a Party rally he had forced himself to attend just before the war started, because he wanted to understand better what was happening in his country. The rally had taken place in a huge oval-shaped *Sportplatz* on the outskirts of the city. The speakers' voices were grotesquely overamplified; as they intensified their rhetoric against the Jews and Gypsies and Communists, they started to shout into the microphone. The thunderous voices echoed throughout the stadium, punctuated by even more thunderous applause and shouting from the thousands of Party faithful gathered there.

The public address system groaned and screeched under the burden of those decibels. All around him, people would leap to their feet in unison whenever a speaker grew vehement in his denunciation of the enemies of the Reich. After a while Keller felt their eyes on him when he stayed in his seat, so he began to yank himself up along with them, though he couldn't bring himself to join in their full-throated hysteria. Of course, he had already understood what was happening to Germany, but now he *felt* it as his body was bombarded by relentless waves of sound.

The speakers drove home their points, slicing the air with exaggerated jabs of their forefingers and sidewise swipes of their fists. Even from a great distance, he could see them going red in the face, their voices rising in pitch as well as volume as the words *Jew, pig, curse, bloodsucker* bounced around the stadium. But the orators and their gestures seemed small against the backdrop of two giant flags emblazoned with swastikas.

After an hour he could no longer concentrate on the speeches; the loudspeakers at the far end of the field fed their words back to his section of the bleachers a second or two after they were spoken, distorting the sense of newer words spewed out by the nearest loudspeaker. He tried to remember all the Jews he'd ever known. Ernst, and Marietta, of course, but other Jews as well—neighbors, acquaintances, colleagues. Not one bore any resemblance to the devils the speakers were describing. But if one of them had been noticed anywhere in the stadium that day, he or she would have been torn apart.

Keller looked to the right and left, down the bleachers and, turning around, up at the rows behind him. He had never seen so many people in this state before. Brown-shirted SA in seats of honor near the field: *their* shouting and fist-shaking came as no surprise. For a few minutes he stared at the backs of their close-cropped heads, their thick, muscular necks. Closer to his seat was a contingent of factory workers from the nearby steel and munitions works, their faces contorted with anger as the speakers spit out *Juden, Zigeuner, Schweine* like clots of phlegm. In the bleachers above him sat a group of Hitler Youth—rosy cheeks, shining eyes, their cherubic faces fired by idealism as the heroic goals of the Reich were enumerated, then flushed and bloated with fury as the names of the enemies who would block those goals were pounded into their brains for the thousandth time.

So here was this Kommandant, an important part of the machine that had been created to deal with the Jews, talking about an attempt to bring them back to life. Maybe he's trying to trap me into saying something unwise, thought Keller. Did the Kommandant know anything about his past? About his friendship with Ernst? But Ernst had left for England in the summer of '33. Or Marietta? But that was a long time ago, too, he reminded himself once again, and it was so brief. Of course, he'd never written a word about her in his diaries. And there hadn't been any other Jewish girls. He had never made any trouble, never said anything that could he held against him.

"Two months ago," continued the Kommandant while Keller was still shuddering at the memory of that rally, "I picked the weakest inmates in the camp—both men and women, about thirty of them. They were fed as normally as possible, housed separately from the other inmates, clothed differently. We encouraged them to move around more freely within their area of the camp, and we let them bathe twice a week."

His eyebrows rose, as if he was impressed by his own generosity.

"Leather shoes were distributed to them, instead of the wood and cloth monstrosities they usually have to patch together. Oh, I'm sorry if this shocks you. We just don't have enough food or clothing to provide adequately for the entire camp."

Keller was sure he had shown no reaction.

"They were given much lighter workloads. The men and women were permitted more contact with each other than usual; eventually they were all put together in one barracks. I wanted to see what effect these new conditions would have on their behavior."

He looked at Keller and paused, as if anxious to reassure himself that the violinist was following every step of his experiment with undivided attention.

He must have noticed my distraction a few minutes ago, thought Keller. Like a schoolteacher. Maybe that's what he was before the war—a professor somewhere, and he misses the classroom as a forum where he can expound his brilliant ideas.

Once again Keller felt he had to make some show of interest. "What changes did you observe, Herr Kommandant?"

"After two weeks their complexions had improved somewhat, and they no longer seemed dazed from hunger. But they were still withdrawn, apathetic . . . even when the guards pushed them around a bit in the course of a day's work."

He snuffed out the cigarette in a heavy glass ashtray, got up from his perch on the desk, walked around it and sat down again in his chair.

Keller glanced at the bookshelves full of Goethe. *Can they ever come back to life from this living death?* Was he trying to be poetic? A touch of Goethe or Schiller, or even Shakespeare, perhaps? Yes, he must have been a professor before the war. A man like him would have needed the stimulation of a university, with all its different disciplines, and the university would have had a laboratory where he could conduct his research.

Now, of course, the Reich had provided him with the perfect place for research—far superior to any university laboratory.

"After a month, though, their behavior became a bit more animated. I admit the change was modest: they still had periods of depression and didn't communicate much with each other. Yet somehow it seemed that they had begun to hope. Their movements weren't as sluggish as usual. As I spoke to the group, I began to notice a—how should I put it?—a certain responsiveness in some of their faces. Nothing specific, just a general level of attention or expectation that was different from before. I'm sure they would have continued to improve, but then . . . one of them tried to escape. They were on their way back from the factory, and it was getting dark. The road skirts some woods—he must have thought it would take only a few seconds to get in there. He didn't seem to know there was a ditch at the side of the road."

He paused, as if for dramatic effect. When he spoke again, his voice was lower in pitch and volume. "He fell into the ditch, and the guards shot him as he was trying to scramble out. If I had been there, I would have stopped them, of course. My chosen ones didn't have much of a reaction at the time, but that one death erased all the hope I had planted in their hearts. Over the next month they became more withdrawn than ever, and ate less, too."

He sighed and shook his head.

"The experiment was at a standstill. For several days I asked myself what could be done to reverse the damage. Then I remembered that the ones who'd lived here in Germany must have had some cultural background. Until a few years ago everything was available to them—theater, poetry readings, concerts. They had their own Kulturbund, you know."

Keller tried to look as if the name of that organization meant nothing to him.

"So I decided to give them music. What better way was there to remind them of their past lives, to kindle in them the hope to live again? Of course, I would have preferred to bring in an orchestra, or a string quartet, or a pianist. But there's no piano here, and I would have had to get one from the city. That would have involved paperwork; it was too complicated. With larger groups there would have been too many people to control effectively. So I had to settle for solo violin."

Keller retreated into his chair, the words *control effectively* resounding in his ears.

"The repertoire is small, but it includes a few of the greatest pieces ever written. I mean the sonatas and partitas of Bach, of course. Ah, I see. You're surprised to find a cultivated man in charge of such a place. But then you have no idea how closely these camps are related to the core of our culture."

He scanned the violinist's face for a reaction to this sweeping statement. All Keller could do was shrug and shake his head slightly, trying to look attentive.

The Kommandant smiled sympathetically. "I understand the needs of artists. What would you say if I told you that the rubber plant will suspend operations while you're here, just because the smell is so overpowering and you're not used to it yet? I don't want anything to distract you from your music. So you see the esteem in which I hold the arts."

"Yes, Herr Kommandant." Keller tried to hide his disgust with the man's posturing. The esteem in which he held the arts seemed as abstract as his theories, and Keller found nothing flattering in it. He hadn't been summoned in order to hear an expression of esteem, he was sure enough of that. He had no idea why a Kommandant would suspend the normal operations of a camp, and couldn't begin to figure out the real reason while he was sitting in this office, listening to speeches.

"Production is important to me, but not as important as the success of my experiment. How many Bach works do you have in your fingers?"

"Three or four."

"And what else?"

"Some Paganini caprices, two sonatas by Ysaÿe, a few pieces by Reger . . ." Keller found himself listing things, unable to respond to the substance of what he had been told. It struck him that he was answering these questions as if he were arranging a series of programs with a concert promoter.

"Do you have anything modern, like Hindemith?" asked the Kommandant, eyeing him intently. "Yes, yes, I know the government has called it degenerate music. But I'm not a pedant. Do you think that what I'm engaged in here is strictly in line with regulations? No—it involves a much broader view of science and life than the usual experiments, which are more . . . anatomical. So, do you have any Hindemith?"

"I know one of the solo sonatas," he admitted.

"Good. Well, that should be enough for about an hour of music each day. This part of the experiment will last four days, during which you'll live in the camp. Oh, don't worry, you won't be treated like the Häftlinge. You'll have a room and bath to yourself, good food and so forth. You'll be allowed to move around the camp freely. Only it would be foolish to let you return to the city each day—too great a security risk."

A security risk? Because of what he had just heard?

"What about after the experiment, Herr Kommandant?"

"After the experiment, you'll understand a great deal more

of this." He made an all-encompassing gesture with one hand, as if to indicate the camp and what it stood for. "You will be different; there will be no security risk."

He didn't say specifically that Keller could leave after four days, but there was no use belaboring that point; it was clear that the Kommandant had no intention of satisfying him with solid assurances. He stood up, looking at his wristwatch and then at the door behind his visitor.

But Keller had one more question. "Excuse me, sir. I suppose you may have conducted some experiments here that might make the layman uneasy, but this one seems less . . ." He tried to think of a neutral word. "Less detached. You seem to be hoping . . ."

"Yes, I'm hoping to reverse the process of decay." There was a dryness, an edge of impatience in his voice. "To prove that it's possible. But instead of wondering about my motives, you would do well to concentrate on your own reasons for being here."

"My own reasons . . ." The only reason Keller could think of was that he had no choice.

"You're a performer: you need an audience as much as I need experimental subjects. Those soldiers you've been playing for—well, it's a nice gesture, but what does it really amount to?"

"I've sometimes wondered the same thing myself."

"Most of them couldn't possibly understand Bach. Soldiers might enjoy hearing Beethoven's Ninth, with its overwhelming power, and some of them might even think they understand it. But a violinist, by himself, trying to pull them into the inner world of Bach?"

A smile spread slowly across his face. He shook his head.

"The nuances would be completely lost upon them when the music doesn't have enough bombast. Now, the Jews, at least the ones who've lived in Germany, have claimed an intimacy with some of our greatest musical treasures. They're Untermenschen, yet they always believed they had a stake in our heritage. That's part of what makes them dangerous: look at the arrogance of Mendelssohn, for example, claiming to be the one who rescued Bach's sacred works from oblivion. But for the time being, it will be to our advantage to revive their illusion of equality."

"I still don't grasp what my own reasons would be for . . ."

"The war has more or less put an end to your normal concert activity, hasn't it? You no longer play for sophisticated German audiences, but you have to stay in shape as a performer. You need to try out your repertoire on the Jews."

"I've never played for prisoners, for people . . . like the Jews you've described. I'm not sure I'll be able to accomplish what you want."

"It won't be easy, but it's the only possible way to bring them back." He moved toward the door. With his hand on the knob, he looked back at Keller as if he had just thought of something. "You must be an Orpheus to them, and thaw their frozen souls."

He seemed impressed by the resonance of his own words as he turned the knob and slowly pulled it.

"I will do my best, Herr Kommandant," Keller stammered. He walked through the doorway. It was only once he got outside and heard the door close behind him that he realized he hadn't been breathing normally for the past half hour. He tried to relax his arms and let his shoulders drop a little. The way he felt now, it would be impossible to play.

At the top of the steps outside he hesitated, looking at the road and the gently sloping fields beyond the barbed-wire enclosure of the camp. It wasn't quite as muddy here as it was nine or ten kilometers back toward the city. There were still some patches of snow that last night's rain had failed to wash away. Here and there a crust of ice glinted under the late morning sun.

Suddenly a long-forgotten scene from childhood came back to him. He was walking in the country with his parents. It must have been late spring; it was already quite warm, and the air was fragrant with the scent of wildflowers. He saw a tiny hole in the ground, out of which big black ants were emerging one by one, at perfectly even intervals. His parents kept walking while he stopped to observe the insects. They seemed to have a destination, or at least an instinctive sense of purpose. That seemed strange, even humorous to him; he couldn't imagine where they were going in such order and harmony. After a while he lifted his foot and stepped firmly on one ant, then on another, and so on. They kept coming. After killing seven or eight of them, he got upset and ran to catch up with his parents.

"Why did they keep coming out?" he asked tearfully. "Why didn't they hide from me?"

IV

It is beyond our comprehension that the immortal German violin concerto of Brahms could be entrusted to a Jew."

The brief review ended with that damning sentence; there was no commentary on the actual playing. He pushed the newspaper back across the table to Ernst. The young man was biting a corner of his lower lip, and his sky-blue eyes locked onto Gottfried's, searching for a reflection of his outrage. Finally he said, "Do you have any idea how this makes me feel?"

"I can imagine. Such filth!" Gottfried looked away from him for a moment and saw an elderly gentleman dining alone in a corner of the café. He was wearing an old-fashioned gray wool suit with a vest and a gold watch chain. He had a high, stiff collar; his hat and cane lay across the table, partly covered by the newspaper he had stopped reading. His gray hair was close-cropped, the hairline receding, and he had a bristly mustache.

"But there are other papers that gave you good reviews," Gottfried said, looking back into Ernst's probing eyes. "This is just an upstart Nazi rag. Do you think a review in here means anything next to the *Kölner Stadt-Anzeiger*?"

"I'm not talking about what the review will do for my career." He shook his head and pursed his lips. "I'm talking about what it means for Germany."

"Kellner!" called the old man in the corner. In his voice there was a note of command that seemed to come naturally. "Rechnung, bitte!" The waiter scurried over and took out his pad, figuring out the bill while the gentleman waited.

They were sitting in the Goldener Adler, the café where Ernst had a job as Kapellmeister, leading and playing solos with a small string orchestra in light classics like Lehár and Johann Strauss, as well as transcriptions of the latest dance tunes and popular songs. He had to do this to support his family, and often joked about the silliness of some of the frothier music he had to play. Gottfried came to the café at least once a week, not only because his best friend was the featured "act." He loved the way it felt to come in there on a cold, rainy evening, or at lunchtime, and be greeted by the smell of stewed meat, fried potatoes, Spiegeleier, and the hum of a dozen conversations.

There were two large rooms besides the kitchen. The inner room had a small stage, but Gottfried didn't spend much time in there because he wasn't interested in light entertainment music. In the outer room the bar, table and chairs were all made of solid oak and mahogany; on the walls were somewhat primitive murals of pastoral and agrarian scenes in faded colors, illustrating old, homey proverbs that were inscribed on the bottom of each tableau in elaborate Gothic lettering.

That afternoon in July 1933, the café was almost empty—4 PM wasn't a peak hour. The other customers were all on the opposite side of the room. They were in Gottfried's peripheral vision as he faced Ernst, and he was only marginally aware of them. Still, as the conversation turned to politics and Ernst's status as a Jew, Gottfried found himself hoping that Ernst and he would be able to keep their voices down. The Party had been in power for five months already, and he regarded it as a hopeful sign that at least they could still talk about politics in a public place rather than having to slink away to one of their homes.

Gottfried glanced once more at the review in the *Völkischer Beobachter*. "Well, what can you do about it?" he asked.

"I'm going to write a letter to the editors, pointing out that Brahms dedicated his immortal German concerto to the Jew, Joseph Joachim, who helped him write the violin part."

"No, Ernst, you're not going to do that."

Ernst nodded his head slowly, the corners of his mouth rising in grim satisfaction. He was drumming softly on the table with his long, tapered fingers. He was an elegant-looking man, even when casually dressed, as he was that day. His blue silk shirt was unbuttoned at the neck, and the wide collar fanned out over the lapels of his jacket. He had full lips, a straight nose, and curly golden-brown hair. Nobody would have guessed he was Jewish. He looked more Aryan than a lot of Germans did, and he was completely assimilated. As far as Gottfried knew, Ernst didn't speak any Yiddish. His family name, Schneider, was neutral: it revealed nothing about his background. Someone had told Gottfried that Ernst was Jewish as he was just getting to know him; otherwise it never would have occurred to him.

He had recently graduated from the Hochschule, where he was one of Professor Kerner's favorite students. Kerner once said to Gottfried, "Ernst is not only one of the most naturally gifted pupils I've had; he has also made the most of his talent. He's a hard worker, and he's got imagination. He absorbs everything I tell him like a sponge, then comes up with something new, all his own." Sometimes Gottfried was jealous of all the attention Ernst got, but then he would remind himself that Ernst was three years older, and more advanced. Besides, Ernst had been encouraging to him about his own playing, enthusiastic even, at times when he needed it. So Gottfried was glad for him when he did well.

For his graduation concert, Ernst had been scheduled to play the Brahms Concerto with the school's top orchestra. In April 1933 a Nazi had been appointed administrative director of the Hochschule, but everyone thought this man was merely a bureaucrat, a token presence installed by the Ministry of Culture. The real power in the school seemed to lie in the hands of the artistic director, Dr. Knapp, a conductor with no obvious political affiliation.

The program for the graduation concert was prominently posted in a glass-encased bulletin board near the entrance. When Ernst arrived at school one day and found his name crossed off the program with a few thick pencil strokes, he suspected and almost hoped it was an expression of resentment by some envious student. But he learned soon enough that his removal from the concert was official. Professor Kerner went with him to the administrative director's office and threatened to resign if Ernst wasn't reinstated on the program. Kerner was important enough to the school for his threat to carry some weight, and with the mediation of Dr. Knapp, a compromise was reached: Ernst would play only the first movement of the Brahms Concerto.

"Ernst," Gottfried said gently, "don't you think you're overreacting a little? When I mentioned those other papers, I wasn't thinking about your career. I was thinking about what's still good and decent and clearheaded in our society. No one I know believes the crap they print in the *Völkischer Beobachter*. Look, there are four well-established papers in this town; two of them gave you good reviews, two gave you raves, and you choose to focus on what some rabid hatemonger has to say."

The old gentleman got up from the table, and Gottfried noticed he was slightly unsteady on his feet as he put on his overcoat. It seemed to be something of a struggle for him to raise his arms high enough to get them into the sleeves. The waiter came over again and helped him. The old fellow indicated his thanks with a stiff nod, then proceeded toward the door. Gottfried was glad to see that the shaky moment had passed, that he was really quite steady once he got moving. The cane was still mostly ornamental; his independence and dignity were still intact.

There was something comforting to him about the elderly man, with his aura of long-settled habits and perhaps more than a hint of pedantry. Was it that he reminded Gottfried slightly of his father? No, it was more than that. This gentleman, probably a retired lawyer or doctor, was a familiar figure: he had seen so many others like him all over the country, in cafés and restaurants, at tram stops, in railroad cars. At concerts. That was why his habits, like the late afternoon beer and cigar over a newspaper in his favorite Stammlokal, felt so comfortable to Gottfried, even though he knew he would never become like that himself. A touring musician couldn't have such settled habits. But he liked having people like that around.

"All I know is that this hatemonger and his rag aren't alone," said Ernst. "Somebody has to send a message to these people—I mean not only the ones who write this trash, but those who read it, too. You may not know anyone who does, but the *Beobachter* has a big circulation."

"You think they'll print it? Next to the editorials, maybe." Gottfried laughed, but when he continued, it surprised him to hear a slight shaking in his voice. "Please don't send that letter, Ernst. It's not a good idea. You never know what might come of a gesture like that; it could come back to haunt you later."

"I'm sniffing a contradiction in your argument. The good and the decent are still by far a majority. I'm making a mountain out of a molehill by paying too much attention to these Nazi crackpots. It doesn't matter that one of them is our chancellor now. The whole thing will blow over—isn't that what you're implying?"

Gottfried shrugged and looked again at the corner table the old man had occupied. The waiter was leaning over it with a dishrag in his right hand, the used plates and beer mug cradled in the crook of his left arm.

"So I shouldn't write the letter because the whole thing isn't important enough to get worked up about. At the same time, you tell me not to write the letter because something bad could happen to me as a result. Do you mean that the newspaper might send some thugs to beat me up? Or that the Nazi state we now have, once its apparatus is securely in place, will take care of me?"

"I . . . I don't know, Ernst, it just doesn't seem like a good idea."

"Either way, it doesn't bode well for our good and decent society, does it? So maybe it is worth getting worked up about, after all. And don't forget that at the concert, the first three rows were filled with the SA in their shit-brown shirts. How do you think it felt to stand in front of the orchestra and look down at those faces of steel? They couldn't believe a Jew would dare play their music."

"You gave a great performance in spite of them."

"Maybe. But how can I keep playing my best from now on, when I know those bastards will be there every time I walk onstage? I was lucky they didn't disrupt the concert. That will come, too, believe me. You know, I teach a little."

Ernst had a way of changing subjects when you least expected it, without a pause for breath. Yet there was always a connection.

"A few months ago one of my pupils came in for his lesson with a swastika armband. It was just before Hitler was elected. I spent the whole hour trying to figure out if he knew I was Jewish, whether this was a deliberate insult or he thought I was a 'good Aryan' who would share his views. It occurred to me that some idiots don't even know the swastika stands for hatred of Jews as well as for the economic recovery they're always talking about. In any case, he's hardly more than a boy, sixteen or so, and what he believes is probably a carbon copy of what his parents believe. Which doesn't make it any better, any less threatening."

"What did you do?"

"Nothing, at first. That's what bothered me. I was furious with myself the whole week until his next lesson. When he walked in again with that filthy thing on his sleeve, I asked him to take it off. He looked at me for a long time without saying anything. I thought his jaw would drop. Then he asked, 'Are you trying to interfere with my right to express myself politically?' He probably figured I'd back down once he expressed that lofty sentiment."

Gottfried laughed. "So he's the champion of freedom of expression, and he's wearing one of those armbands! I gather you didn't back down."

"No, I didn't. I put it to him like this: 'Normally I wouldn't interfere with any of your rights. It's just that this offends me personally.'

"He kept staring at me, and I had the feeling that he was

really seeing me for the first time, not just as his violin teacher but as a person. Then I saw him swallow before he spat this out: 'So . . . are you a Jew-lover?'"

With those words, Ernst's imitation of his student's voice turned into a high-pitched, singsong whine. Gottfried was glad that his friend wasn't mimicking the boy too loudly; he didn't want him to attract any attention to their table. Not while they were talking about this subject.

"Well, by that time it could hardly have been much of a surprise for you," he said. "It must have been disgusting, though, to hear that kind of filth coming from a youngster you thought you knew. How can one respond to a question like that?"

"I just moved toward the door. My hand was on the knob, and then I turned and looked back at him. You know, at that moment I really hated him, with his perfect straight blond hair always slicked down. I remembered the whole year of lessons we'd had. I hated the way he held his head, the way his jaw jutted so squarely over the chinrest when he played. I hated his pedantic accuracy, hated even the progress he'd made because it was all technical. His phrasing never improved, no matter what I said."

Ernst grimaced and shook his head, as if he was hearing the boy's scrapings all over again. "If it could even be called 'phrasing.' Stiff as a board. But most of all I hated that dry tone of his, which I hadn't been able to change. Vibrato exercises, working on smooth bow changes, getting him to listen to singers—all useless."

Ernst had always seemed so calm, so self-assured in a modest way, that he didn't need to criticize anyone else. This was one of the qualities that had drawn Gottfried to him: he rose above the gossip and occasional backstabbing that pep-

pered the usual conversations at the Hochschule. It disturbed
the younger man now to hear him put down his student like
that. He felt a sudden impulse to defend the boy, even though
he abhorred his politics.

"His sense of music-making was more appropriate for a
marching band than for a violinist," Ernst added. "For some
reason I held myself back from saying so, even at that moment."

Gottfried's mouth was dry; he needed a refill of his beer,
but the waiter was nowhere to be found. He turned all the way
around in his chair, but Ernst went on, oblivious to the fact
that his friend's back was turned to him.

"Why I should have acted with any consideration for his
feelings, I'll never know. All I said was, 'If I have any self-
esteem, then I must be a Jew-lover.' I yanked the door open so
hard that he jumped. Then he left, without another word."

Gottfried gave up on the waiter and swiveled around to
face Ernst again. "You handled it the right way."

"I don't think so. Not exactly. I should've done something
the first time."

"But you were caught off guard. You needed time to think
it over, to figure out how to respond."

"I don't think there will always be time for people to think
things over in the years ahead. Anyway, I have thought it over
since the last time I saw him, and what disturbs me most of all
in this little story is what it has shown me about myself. How
passive I must be if I can't respond decisively to bigotry in a
student, in a situation where I'm the authority and should be
in control! I'm just like all the rest of the good, decent people
who won't speak up or act while there's still time."

"You're being too hard on yourself, Ernst."

"The first lesson when that clown wore the armband, I

didn't know whether or not to tell him I was Jewish. Even when I kicked him out, I couldn't say it directly. I was clinging to my Germanness and hiding the truth about myself. In front of an untalented pupil! My God, how would I act when it's the authorities I'm facing? Especially when they're trying to take away my right to be German?"

He had managed to keep his voice from rising, but with the last words he swatted the Nazi paper onto the floor and clenched his fist as if he was going to pound the table. Gottfried looked at the people drinking and chatting at a few tables alongside the opposite wall. They hadn't noticed anything yet.

Ernst seemed to be aware of his discomfort. He spread out his fingers and said quietly, "Don't worry. I won't make a scene. It might come back to haunt you or me later on."

"Please, Ernst. I'm your friend—I hope one of your best friends. Don't become bitter toward all Germans."

"I'm sorry. I won't. How can I, anyway, when I'm as much a German as any of you?"

Gottfried was about to protest, thinking Ernst had mistaken his meaning when he said the words *all Germans*—of course, he hadn't meant to exclude him—but Ernst held up his hand. "I know you meant no harm. You are a good friend. Please don't take it personally if I'm upset."

But the expression on his face didn't match the conciliatory words. His mouth was set in a narrow, rigid mold, and his eyes seemed to focus on some imaginary point a few feet behind his friend. Gottfried began to feel like he wasn't really there for Ernst, like he was just being used as a sounding board.

"Listen, there's one more thing I have to tell you. You know my brother Gerhard, don't you? Half a year ago he started working for an engineering firm. Since last week there's a new company policy: the official greeting when answering the telephone is supposed to be 'Heil Hitler!' My brother won't say this, and I don't think he'll last long there. He and I are getting out, anyway. Professor Kerner has given me letters of recommendation to all his contacts in England. I don't want to give myself any more chances to react passively. I'm not waiting for what might happen here."

He downed what remained in his beer mug with a defiant gulp. To Gottfried's dismay he found himself disliking Ernst for the first time. There was a coldness in Ernst's anger that made him feel excluded because he happened to be an Aryan.

Over the next few days, Gottfried wondered if Ernst had been cold to him because he couldn't tune himself up to the proper pitch of indignation about the review in the *Völkischer Beobachter*. He thought he'd been contemptuous enough of the critic and the whole newspaper. Had he been too optimistic about the state of affairs in Germany? He didn't know exactly what Ernst had expected of him, or what he should have done differently, but it was clear that much had changed between them that afternoon.

The following week he was one of a small circle of friends who saw Ernst off at the Hauptbahnhof. Afterward he received two postcards and eventually some letters, in which Ernst dwelt on details of his new life, with no mention of the tense moments they had spent at the café. Things seemed to be going well for him in London, but every time Gottfried thought of him, he felt sad. They could avoid the subject in the letters they exchanged; on the surface they could back away from a total estrangement, but the fact was that their last afternoon together had chilled the feeling of friendship between them. With Ernst in England, they might never see each other again.

V

Toward four o'clock, a guard appeared at the door of Keller's room and led him to the area where the prisoners were kept. This was separated from the Kommandant's office and the guards' quarters by an internal barbed-wire fence. They entered a one-story brick building that consisted of a single large room with several rows of low, backless benches. Nobody else was there yet. The windows were small and dirty, letting in only a fraction of the already meager late afternoon light. There was no heat, and he was already wondering how to get some blood circulating to his fingers. As he was unpacking his violin, the Kommandant came in and said that he would introduce him to the inmates.

They entered a few moments later, slowly, one by one. Eight or ten guards accompanied them, taking up positions alongside the walls.

Barely human, the way they move, the way they look. My God, what's happened to them?

And these were the ones who'd been fed "normally" for the past few weeks. He tried to picture them as they might have looked before, tried to *see* them in their various lives before they were wrenched from their homes and brought here. It was impossible.

He remembered cheerful, plump Frau Nierenberg, his next-door neighbor while he was studying in Cologne. She occasionally invited him in for coffee and cakes, said she liked the sound of his practicing. Her teenage daughter, Rachel, a thinner, paler version of her mother, used to refill his cup and plate but always seemed slightly shy in his presence.

Where were they now? They had nothing to do with these people.

Pressure was building behind his eyes. He had to look away.

He had imagined the inmates living in squalor, but was unprepared for the stench that enveloped him as soon as they were assembled—something like cheese that had been left standing around too long, he thought, or rancid butter, tinged with that bittersweet scent from the smokestacks.

That's the only drawback. It gets in your hair, your clothes, flavors the food you eat.

Within a few days he would probably smell like that.

The price one has to pay for progress.

He swallowed hard a few times, trying to clear his mouth of the bitter saliva that was filling it. He stared at the door and wondered if they'd ever let him out. Then he looked at the Kommandant, who was studying him, impervious to the sight of those phantoms.

"You may sit down," he said in a dry, neutral voice, barely glancing at the prisoners.

Most of them dropped onto the benches with obvious relief, but two remained standing quite close to Keller, looking straight ahead. They seemed not to have heard the Kommandant's words—or maybe the invitation to sit hadn't

sounded enough like an order. Those two didn't seem to notice Keller, but the blackened hollows beneath their eyes were
staring at him.

One of the guards came over and led them to a bench a
few steps away. They turned their heads slightly but did not
quite look at him as he ushered them along, barely touching
their sleeves with the tips of his gloved fingers, as if he dreaded
contamination through direct contact with those subhuman
creatures.

"Today, and for the next three days," began the Kommandant in a slightly warmer tone, "I have a special program for
you." He began to walk slowly around the room, between the
guards and the prisoners, his hands clasped behind his back.
"You have not experienced anything like it since your arrival
here. This young man will play the violin for you." He indicated Keller with one hand, but most of them didn't look at
him; some were staring at the floor, others at the walls.

They didn't seem to mind the closeness in there, the lack
of air.

It would have been easier to face a row of corpses in a
morgue, thought Keller. He would have only had to look—not
play, not try to move them. Then he could have left, and
gulped some air.

Looking away, he tried to loosen his grip on the violin. He
was clutching it so tightly that he'd never be able to play well
once the Kommandant was finished with his introduction.
And he was holding the bow like a club. He managed to trans-
fer the violin to his right hand, then opened and closed his left
fist behind his back a few times in an attempt to stretch the
stiffness and cold out of his fingers.

"He is very good," continued the Kommandant, "and already has achieved some distinction in his career. Recently he

has been playing for our wounded soldiers near the battle-front. That is his contribution to the war effort."

As the Kommandant spoke, Keller's eyes returned to the mass of gray in front of him—gray, shroudlike garments, gray complexions, gray scalps from which the hair had been shorn. Some of them looked back at him now. He could have been a wall, or another guard; it didn't matter. When their eyes met, he averted his. What struck him most was that they all looked so much alike, at least at first glance. The entire group seemed to be around the same age, but that could have been anywhere from twenty to fifty. And in that half-light it was difficult to tell the difference between men and women. If he was looking at women, he couldn't see the contours of their bodies.

"He is here now to help you renew your sense of beauty, which you have lost. For his presence you may thank the Third Reich."

The Kommandant smiled broadly at him. His eyes held Keller's for several seconds as the smile faded from his face. Then his glasses caught a momentary shaft of sunlight—he was standing next to a window—and the glare of the reflection made the violinist look away.

Keller had chosen to begin with some Paganini caprices, the most purely virtuosic music in his repertoire. Grab their attention, banish their listlessness with dazzling effects. Earlier that day, as he was hurriedly putting together some pieces for the first concert, this seemed to be a better approach than starting with a deeper, more introspective work—a mistake he had often made with the soldiers. Bach's music would require his listeners to be already attuned to fine shades of meaning, to enter a world of subtleties without transition from their bru-tal, deadening existence.

But avoiding one mistake was no guarantee against making another: he wasn't used to starting his programs with virtuoso pieces. Keller knew that it would be easier to tackle the pyrotechnics once he'd gotten past his nervousness and given his muscles a chance to loosen up. Having played these caprices dozens of times in hospitals, though, he felt he could take the risk of starting with them.

First he played Caprice Number Nine in E Major, a sparkling piece in which double-stopped thirds, fifths and sixths imitate the sound of hunting horns. He'd had great success with this caprice in his graduation recital at the Hochschule. Other students had told him afterward how much they admired the clearly chiseled scales and double-stops, but the memory of that triumph was clouded by more recent performances for the wounded soldiers, who barely reacted to his attempts at virtuosity.

In fairness to the soldiers, though, his playing was no longer the same as it had been ten years earlier. These days it was hard for him to work up any enthusiasm when he took his violin out of its case every morning to begin practicing. There was no freshness in his work anymore, no belief that it would lead anywhere, least of all to progress. The best he could do nowadays was to try to recapture what he had lost.

The lighthearted opening theme of the Ninth Caprice alternates with more dramatic sections in minor keys. There are fistfuls of chords, rapid scales in the high register and a passage of ricochet, a special technique in which the bow is thrown onto the string to produce a series of rebounding notes. In order to run this gamut of difficulties successfully, one's hands must be absolutely limber. Before he started to play, Keller hoped against all reason that this one time he would be exempt, that it might still sound good enough for him to walk through that door at the end of the "concert" with a modicum of self-respect.

Missed notes, garbled ricochet, scratchy chords. He told himself it was still decent, even though it was far from his best playing. But was it good enough? If these people had really been concertgoers when they were free, they would know what great playing was like. He tried to stay rational, optimistic, to give himself a chance to adjust to the situation—if not today, then by tomorrow. But deep down he was disturbed by the very first sounds he produced, and this feeling refused to go away.

His fingers ached; as he made his way through the Ninth Caprice and began the next one, each upcoming challenge loomed as an insurmountable hurdle. After ruining one of the more treacherous passages, he had to keep himself from stopping in the middle of the piece. He'd spent too many hours of his life practicing those scales and double-stops to be able to bear such a performance. He could almost hear himself say, *The hell with it!*—could imagine the silence that would follow those words as he packed up his violin and got out of there. That would be humiliating, but he had already lost face through his playing. It seemed impossible to disgrace himself any further, and besides, who cared what these people thought of him? They'd probably be dead in a week.

What they needed was food, not music, and it made a mockery of his music to pretend otherwise, to make believe that this pigsty was a concert hall where people could concentrate on anything besides the growling in their bellies.

They all sat motionless; they might as well have been dead already. Something about their shoulders—he thought he could see the bones sticking out through their clothes—made him want to grab them and shake them. But then he remembered that no audience could see him from inside, the way he saw himself. These people most likely saw and heard nothing. Why should he admit defeat in front of the Kommandant, who for all his air of culture and sophistication might be tone-deaf?

And in his struggles with the Paganini, he'd almost forgotten: There was more at stake than his self-respect as a violinist. He had been brought here to play, and he couldn't refuse to do the Kommandant's bidding.

So he finished the second of his caprices. There was one more to go: Number Five in A Minor, which under normal circumstances could be dazzling. It opens with a series of arpeggios from the low to the high registers, each one followed by a scale hurtling down. Then comes a moto perpetuo, to be played as fast as possible, with precise articulation on every note.

This had been a warhorse of his in the early years after his graduation from the Hochschule. Suddenly he could remember the exhilaration of performing this caprice with flair, could feel once again the joy of watching his fingers work as efficiently as pistons, knowing that he had pushed the tempo to the limit. If for one moment he let up his concentration, or became self-conscious, the whole thing could spin out of control. But that had never happened. After all these years he could still hear the gasp of amazement from the audience when he came to the end. That gasp had meant even more to him than the rush of applause that followed.

He shut his eyes in order to block out the misery in front of him, and played this one better than the other caprices. By now there was some blood flowing in his fingers. He took more chances, and even made a bravura gesture on the final chord: he held his bow up high for a moment, the scroll of his violin pointing toward the ceiling.

Silence. Absolute silence.

Slowly he brought down the bow and opened his eyes. Only then did the Kommandant begin to applaud. His hands made a dry, solitary sound in the dead acoustics of the room. He cleared his throat and said, "Clap." His voice sounded distant, as if he was preoccupied with other matters.

Perhaps they hadn't heard him.

"Clap," he repeated, a bit louder. "The man has performed for you, and you must show your appreciation."

Two or three started to bring their hands together in a slow, noiseless imitation of the Kommandant.

"Clap!" he yelled.

The guards began to move toward the prisoners. Only then did they all make the required noise—each one sporadically, the total sound unsynchronized and thin. The guards returned to their places along the wall without having touched the inmates; the Kommandant, seemingly satisfied with the paltry courtesy he had extracted from the audience, left the building without looking at him.

Keller bowed. The applause continued mechanically; it proved as difficult to turn off as it had been to turn on. He tuned for the next piece while they were still clapping—the ovation wasn't loud enough to prevent him from hearing himself. He got ready to play, but their hands still came together with grim regularity as they stared straight ahead. He brought down his violin and looked around, not knowing what to do. Finally a guard stamped his foot, just once, and there was silence.

The second piece he had planned was a sonata by the great Belgian violinist Eugène Ysaÿe. Ysaÿe's works demand virtuosity, but always in the service of musical ideas and atmosphere. The Fifth Sonata is in two movements, "L'Aurore" and "Danse

Rustique." In "L'Aurore," the delicate tints of spring emerge from the obscurity of night. The rising sun, represented by a theme woven into a tapestry of arpeggios, grows in intensity until it reaches a radiant climax.

He had once performed this piece at an exhibition of French Impressionist paintings in Cologne. It was during his second or third year at the Hochschule, when he was still carefree enough to immerse himself in some of those seductive canvases before the concert, fascinated by the brushwork and the warm, rich colors that seemed to dominate every other element—the lines, the perspective, the composition.

Practicing the Ysaÿe, he had hoped that this wash of color would soothe and delight the reawakened senses of the prisoners. As he began to actually play the sonata, his only wish was to get through it with as few mishaps as possible and to be done with the whole performance for that day. He no longer thought of trying to please those people; he wasn't crazy enough to believe he could.

It took him until the "Danse Rustique" to realize just what had happened after the Paganini; the silence had numbed him. No performance of his had ever been greeted with silence, not even when he played for the soldiers. And then that applause! It was a mockery, worse than silence. The guards could have stopped it sooner, but he was convinced they let it go on as long as possible just to humiliate him. They themselves didn't clap at all, because the Kommandant's order wasn't directed at them. They'd be damned if *they* would clap with the Jews.

Finishing the Ysaÿe, he expected the same idiotic routine, perhaps with a guard giving the order instead of the Kommandant. But the prisoners started clapping right away—still an unenthusiastic dribble of applause, yet they didn't have to be forced. Keller wondered why. Maybe they were more afraid of the guards when the Kommandant wasn't around to restrain them; a second silence might be interpreted as disobedience to the order they had already received.

Then he hit upon a more convincing explanation: the Kommandant had turned the key in his mechanical puppets by yelling "Clap!" Though at first they were a bit rusty, by now they could do a passable imitation of one example of human behavior. This time the applause even died away after a suitable period.

Keller continued to play his role in the mechanical ritual; like the Jews, he had no choice. His next and last piece for the day was the Partita in E Major by Bach, the most accessible of the master's six works for unaccompanied violin. It starts with a brilliant prelude, full of spirals and cascades of running notes, followed by five dance movements. The whole partita, though richly varied in tempo and character, is full of joy.

Now Keller understood that it probably made no difference how he played or how they reacted. Only there was a slight chance that if the playing was good enough, it might produce some hints of life in his listeners. Not pleasure, not understanding, just . . . a response to a stimulus. He wasn't sure what that would mean to the Kommandant, other than achieving the immediate goal of his bizarre experiment. An idea began to take root, though, while he was playing the graceful, poignant Loure: if music had the power to revive, the Kommandant might not want to send these people back to their "living death" once the experiment was over. Not that he cared about them; Keller couldn't let himself believe that even for a moment. But wouldn't he be proud of his results? Wouldn't he want those results to last?

There was no way to know. His job was simply to make it

through the next few days, give the man what he wanted and get out of there. If he had to muffle his reactions, had to deaden his brain and heart in order to do what was required, so be it.

Anyway, I won't become like them, he thought, half-opening his eyes and taking in the rows of gray, blocklike forms in front of him. But if he did or said anything out of line—surely the guards would report every detail of his behavior—the Kommandant could easily keep him there as long as he liked. Who outside the camp would know?

Looking back on this performance, Keller would have been hard pressed to say how he played the Bach. Did he convey any of its joy? Unlikely. The best he could do here was to adjust to the situation, not rise above it. And he could forget about trying to play as well as he used to.

He was so wrapped up in his thoughts and worries that he let the partita play itself, without listening too much. The final notes came as a relief: his ordeal was finished, at least for that day. He bowed three or four times and forced a smile in response to the dull applause, then turned away to put the violin in its case.

When he turned back, they were still sitting there, as if awaiting further orders. The guards were motionless. Keller cleared his throat and spoke. "That was the end of today's concert; thank you very much for your attention." He hesitated, scanned their faces. "If you have any questions about the music, I would be happy to answer them." He often said something like this at the beginning of his hospital appearances. Here, though, he had simply announced the pieces before playing them. Further explanations seemed unnecessary, or useless. He didn't really expect these people to ask anything.

After a few seconds he picked up his violin and took a couple of steps toward the door. Suddenly a toneless, broken voice pierced the stillness.

"Why did you come here?"

Keller stopped and turned around. He couldn't see who had asked the question; it was getting dark, and the voice had come from somewhere in the back of the room.

"Why did I come here?" he repeated, looking from one expressionless face to another. Was the question hostile or simply curious? "I'm here to bring you music . . . to give you pleasure . . . to help you." His voice dropped with the last few words; he himself could barely hear them.

"I . . ." He should have left before opening his mouth again, but stood there transfixed until the real answer came stammering out. "I was ordered to come here."

———————

Shortly after Keller was escorted back to his room, he forced himself to open the violin case and tried to practice the next day's repertoire. Tomorrow he had to do better; otherwise it would be hard to live with himself. But he was much too tired to get anything done. He lay down on the narrow bed and dozed off for half an hour.

Emerging from sleep, he felt like he had to fight his way back to the surface from the depths of a pit. He groped for the light switch on the wall. Squinting, trying to reorient himself, he looked around the room—at the single plain, hard chair, the unvarnished wood of the desk at the foot of the bed, the grayish paint chipping and peeling from the upper walls. He shivered, and glanced at the window to see if it was open a crack. During the concert he'd longed for nothing so much as some fresh air. Now, in his room, he was afraid a draft was seeping in from somewhere, carrying with it the smell from the chimneys. He sniffed a few times, then decided it was just his imagination.

A guard brought his dinner at seven o'clock, without a word. After the door closed behind him, Keller stared at the tray. There was a plate of sauerbraten with red cabbage, a bowl of spätzle and a carafe of red wine. It wasn't gourmet fare—the meat was overcooked and dry. But it must have been better than what the prisoners were getting, even the Kommandant's chosen ones.

The memory of that smell from the rubber plant was an unwelcome seasoning to his food; he had no appetite, yet forced himself to eat a little. After dinner there was nothing for him to do, no books to read, no way to take his mind off the gloom of the camp.

That night he dreamt he was playing a concert in a large hall that was very dimly lit. Only thirty or forty people were scattered through the first few rows, and beyond that he could hardly see anything.

He felt no response from the audience as he played; they didn't seem to be listening. He expected them to start coughing or shuffling in their seats, but they didn't move. It wasn't as if he had them spellbound, either. God, no—his playing didn't warrant it.

He stopped in the middle of a phrase, to see if that would have any effect. "Are you deaf?" he shouted.

No response. He came down from the stage and approached a cluster of people, grabbed one of them by the shoulders and shook him. Since only the stage was lit, it was too dark for him to see the man's face. Crouching, leaning forward, he could make out a pair of lusterless eyes staring at him. He touched the man's cheek. It was ice cold.

"This man is dead!" he whispered. He looked around and

repeated those words, his voice rising, but there was still no answer.

A woman was huddled in a seat not far away, her face covered by a veil. He pulled away the veil and a skull grinned at him. He jumped back, gagging on the dust he'd stirred up, then ran down the aisle. They started to move, grabbing at him with icy fingers. He turned and bolted back toward the stage, scrambled up the side steps, pushed and pulled and banged at the door that led to the wings.

Retreating toward the center of the stage, he saw his violin and bow on a chair. He picked up the instrument and tried to play again, his hands shaking uncontrollably. At the first notes he woke up.

Oh God, where am I?

He staggered out of bed and pulled open the door, gasping for air. A gust of freezing wind took his breath away.

The light of dawn was gray, metallic, just enough for him to see row after row of low, drab buildings, all exactly alike with a sort of no-man's-land between each row. He longed for the narrow streets of his town, could almost cry when he pictured his little apartment, with its familiarity and modest comforts.

There was barbed wire not far from his door—the internal fence that separated the administrative buildings from the prisoners' barracks. As the wind buffeted him, he stared at the patches of frost on the uneven ground, wondering what this place had looked like before they built that monstrous grid.

Through the wire he saw a cluster of inmates emerging from one of the barracks a few hundred feet away, herded, prodded along by a few guards. Then another barracks spewed out its human stuffings, then a third, and so on until the whole area was a sea of striped uniforms, a tide of automatons moving slowly toward the main gate.

When they stopped in the Appellplatz for roll call, the guards counted and re-counted each row of prisoners. A burly Oberscharführer strutted back and forth between the rows, barking at the cowering inmates for half an hour about God knew what. From time to time he interrupted his harangue to shove or hit those standing closest to him. Then he would place his hands on his hips and plant his feet far apart, triumphantly watching them totter and fall like toothpicks. Whenever the Oberscharführer tapped his thigh with the truncheon he was holding, one of his underlings would run over and kick the fallen inmate until he managed to pull himself up.

Keller wondered if he was still in the throes of his dream.

A sudden blast of noise made him jump, but the guards and prisoners had no reaction. Music? From where? He looked up and saw four loudspeakers towering over the Appellplatz. Could that be a waltz crackling through the static? A spirited accompaniment to this brutality?

During that endless roll call, waltzes, fox-trots and tangos blared from the speakers. The music was so loud that the simple melodies were blurred and grossly distorted: Everything ran together in a merry-go-round of shrill gaiety. Only the highest overtones could cut through the static and the Oberscharführer's shouting.

Suddenly he recognized a tune that Ernst had often played at the Goldener Adler. Dear, fiery Ernst. He had seen it all so clearly in 1933 and had gotten out. Thank God. Or he would have ended up in a place like this, absorbing insults and blows, hopelessly waiting for deliverance from this nightmare.

He had the good sense to leave, but what about me? Why

*didn't I see this coming? And how in God's name have I ended up
here, in this place meant for Gypsies and Jews?*

———————

The roll call was over, and the tide of shadow-creatures had
been shoved through the gate. He leaned out of the doorway
and breathed deeply, trying to calm himself. The smoke that
had hovered over the camp yesterday was no longer visible;
nothing was coming out of the chimneys, but the smell was
still there.

Suddenly it became clear: the main purpose of this place
couldn't be the work it was extracting from those wretched
people. They would work a lot faster and better if they weren't
treated like this.

A thin layer of soot coated his window. He passed one
hand across the glass, then stood there a few moments, staring
at his blackened fingertips.

VI

W ith respect, Herr Kommandant . . ."

"You haven't slept well, I see."

Keller hesitated.

"Did you have bad dreams?"

He knows.

Had someone been looking through his window as he slept? Had he cried out? Or were the dreams a normal part of life here?

"I had a rough night." His head ached, his mouth was dry. The Kommandant waited for him to continue, shuffling some papers on his desk.

Perhaps there was still time to make up some pretext for having come to his office.

"You may speak freely," said the Kommandant, glancing at him over the rims of his glasses. He scribbled a note in the margin of one of the sheets he was holding.

Keller was tempted to change course—to ask for advice about what he should play that afternoon, thank the Kommandant and return to his room. But ever since the roll call a few hours earlier, he'd had only one thought: to find some way to convince this man to let him go. He couldn't face those people again.

"May I ask, sir . . . is this only a labor camp?"

The Kommandant looked up quickly from his papers. His eyes held Keller's until the violinist had to look away; he could tell that the Kommandant knew what he was really asking. There was neither confirmation nor denial in his face, neither guilt nor pride. Just a matter-of-fact, slightly bored expectation, as if he was trying to gauge what Keller might do next.

"I told you all you needed to know," he said finally. "We put them to work here."

"But I can't understand . . . why they look like that."

"I said yesterday, conditions are brutal and not everyone can survive."

"Yes. At first I thought, if some of them died, it was due to the harsh conditions you described—the hunger and cold, the hard labor. That's what I believed, until I saw them."

"And then?"

I've started down this path. I can't turn back now.

"Then . . . I remembered what you said about the necessity of separating the Jews from the rest of us, to avoid contamination. I began to wonder what happens to them after they've been here awhile. I mean, when they're no longer able to work."

The Kommandant's face hardened slightly. "And what did you come up with?"

"Isn't it true, Herr Kommandant, that one of the purposes of this camp"—he paused, searching for an indirect way to put it, then gave up and plunged forward—"is to get rid of these people?"

"How did you arrive at this conclusion?" His lips barely moved as he spoke.

Keller didn't dare mention the endless roll call, the Oberscharführer's shouting and shoving, the hideous music.

"They wouldn't look like that otherwise, they wouldn't *act* like that if they had any hope."

"I see. Well, you're a very acute observer." He put down the papers he was holding, took off his glasses and leaned forward, almost halfway across his desk. "What are you going to do about it?"

Keller pulled back under the pressure of his stare. His heart was racing, and he wanted to make sure his voice wouldn't shake when he responded. "I'm not going to do anything *about* it. It's just that I can't perform well under these circumstances. I wasn't trained for it, and I don't think I'll be able . . . to give you what you want."

"Ah, an aesthetic problem. And an ethical one, too, I suppose."

"Herr Kommandant, you yourself said yesterday that an artist can't do his best when he is merely following orders."

For a moment the Kommandant seemed amused to hear his own words offered back to him. "Well, I must admit I'm disappointed for the experiment. I thought it had a lot of potential. Of course, you won't be kept here against your will." He paused a few seconds. "I gather this is a request to leave."

Keller remained silent; all morning he'd been worrying about the consequences of making such a request.

"I'll instruct the guards to open the gate for you immediately. Only, you should bear in mind that we live in a state of martial law, since it is wartime. The security of the Third Reich comes before everything; the Gestapo sees to that. People are often arrested for no apparent reason."

Keller took a deep breath and tried again to keep his voice steady. "You mean I might be arrested if I leave?"

The Kommandant shrugged his shoulders.

"But I present no threat to the security of the Third Reich."

"You have seen this place."

"Nothing I've seen would compromise . . ."

"Look, you don't seem to understand the opportunity you have here. Patriotic services performed at a camp like this could go a long way toward erasing any suspicions that the authorities might have about you."

"Suspicions? Why should I be under suspicion?"

"Oh, most people have something in their past that can be dug up when necessary."

Marietta. It had to be her. Or maybe Ernst, with his damned letter to the editor of the *Völkischer Beobachter.*

The Kommandant looked down at the papers on the desk and began to busy himself with them again. "There's another thing, too," he added after a few moments. "I am obligated to write a periodic report about everything that goes on here, including unusual events like your concerts. It seems that you don't approve of the camp. I'm afraid I'll have to mention that."

"Approve of it, Herr Kommandant?"

Those eyes were fixed on him again.

"It's not that I'm against what's being done here," Keller heard himself say. "I wouldn't presume to question the judgment of our leaders, to know better than they what's best for the German people."

"If you decline to participate in the experiment, no matter how I characterize that, it will be interpreted as disapproval of the camp. So perhaps you'll reconsider and stay."

Keller sank back in his chair.

"You'll be surprised at how quickly you get used to it. Besides, it seems to me you'd have your own reasons for wanting to stay—under a pretense of unwillingness, of course. The experiment suits your purposes."

"My purposes?" It took an effort to keep his voice from rising.

"You must admit it's a tremendous challenge. To kill them is easy, of course. But to bring them back to life . . . that's something I couldn't do alone. So I yield to your talent. Think of it, the power of life and death over your audience. Not in the usual sense of the phrase: I mean power of life and death *in both directions.* To bring death or to grant new life. That's what I'm offering, even though you'll claim you want nothing to do with the first half."

As the Kommandant spoke, Keller thought of the automatons he'd played for the day before, their pallid, parchmentlike skin, the brittle bones just beneath. And then the corpses in his dream—the lifeless eyes, the empty sockets, the bony grip of their fingers.

He got up and made for the door, then forced himself to look back, to see if the Kommandant had anything further to say.

But the Kommandant was silent; he was staring at the wall behind Keller, who turned around to find himself face-to-face with a portrait of Hitler in full uniform, standing on a rocky plateau in gloves and a billowing cape, looking heroic against a background of dark clouds rent by lightning. Next to the oil painting was a framed page from a "German War Christmas" album, with an inspirational message from the Führer in elegant Gothic script beneath a spray of flowers: "All nature is a gigantic struggle between strength and weakness, an eternal victory of the strong over the weak."

When Keller pulled open the door, the guard waiting at the end of the corridor turned his head sharply. Keller forced a look of calm onto his face, hesitated a moment, then left the building and made his way alongside the internal barbed-wire fence toward his little cell of a room. He wanted to get his violin and get the hell out of there, but he felt the energy and determination draining out of him as he thought of what the Kommandant had said about the Gestapo. His pace slowed; by the time he got to his room, he was very tired.

He sat down on the bed. After a few minutes he got up and grabbed his instrument, but stopped at the door, staring at its crudely fitted planks. He backed away and sat down again, brooding on what he had seen and heard.

The Kommandant's meaning was clear enough. He didn't want him just following orders, but he'd have to report him if he didn't stay and do as he was told. Not just obediently: willingly, cheerfully, with commitment. He understood the needs of artists, but he expected Keller to do his best—on command.

Once again Keller picked up his violin, and once again he hesitated at the door. It would be dangerous to leave before the experiment was over, but it might also be dangerous to stay. This time he turned the knob and, without any clear idea of what he should do, headed toward the main gate.

He could see the Kommandant speaking with a group of guards as he approached. Within the group he noticed two men in long leather coats. His throat tightened when he remembered that the Gestapo didn't always wear uniforms. One of the men took a final puff of a cigarette, tossed it to the ground and stepped on it with a leisurely swiveling motion as he looked around the camp. The other, holding a briefcase, nodded slightly in response to something the Kommandant was saying. Keller veered away from the gate and walked as calmly as he could toward a cluster of warehouses not far away.

He slipped behind the corner of a warehouse and waited for his heartbeat to slow down. He was sure they had been talking about him.

Keller peered through a grimy window, expecting to see crates or sacks piled up against the walls. There was nothing inside but a thick layer of shoes carpeting the floor—hundreds, no, thousands of them. *Leather shoes.* Men's, women's, children's. Mostly simple walking shoes, but also a sprinkling of sandals, heavy boots and house slippers. Some were in good condition, but most of them were dried out, dusty, weatherbeaten, shapeless, a mute chorus of gaping mouths.

I'm sorry if this shocks you. We just don't have enough food or clothing to provide adequately for the entire camp.

How many layers of lies and half-truths would he have to peel away before he understood what was going on here? He stared at the other warehouses nearby, wondering what else had been plundered from those people.

He could see a small group of inmates just beyond the gate, hauling sacks onto a train. A whistle blew; doors were pulled shut, and a caravan of five or six freight cars started to move away from the loading platform. As the train picked up speed, Keller began to guess at some gigantic process of exchange grinding on from day to day, linking this camp to the world outside.

Uproot them, enslave them, murder them, and recycle their possessions back into the economy of the Reich. It's wartime, after all; we're stretched to our limits; we need everything we can lay our hands on. And let's not forget to experiment on some of them before it's too late.

The Gestapo agents, still surveying the camp as they spoke to the Kommandant, walked with him toward his office. Before anyone could see Keller, he turned around and hurried back to his room. He put his violin case on the bed, opened it, and stared at the instrument for a few minutes. Its reddish-orange varnish glowed seductively, even in the harsh, un-shaded electric light of that room. He picked it up. It was so beautiful, the only thing of beauty he'd seen since his arrival there. He turned it around several times; as usual, the back of the violin took his breath away, with its gorgeous deep red flames converging on the center seam. Then he looked out the window, barely able to believe that those hideous barracks beyond the fence were made of the same material as his violin.

He had a lot of practicing to do, and the day passed quickly. It was pretty quiet, at least in that corner of the camp. He needed those scales and arpeggios, needed the methodical buildup of difficult passages from slow to fast tempos. He tried to remember everything his teachers had taught him before the insanity started, tried to recall everything he'd learned on his own. He had to forget where he was. After all, what could he do to change any of it?

VII

He first met her in a theory and solfège class at the Hochschule, in the fall of '34. He hadn't noticed her yet by the second session—she was sitting in the back of the room—but when the professor called on her to sight-sing a Bach chorale, she responded with a bell-like voice. Not the trained voice of a singing student. It didn't have that kind of fullness, or the self-consciousness of trying to produce a perfect sound, or the other kind of self-consciousness that most of the instrumentalists had because their voices sounded so bad. No, it was a naturally beautiful voice, light, transparent, perfectly in tune. But it wasn't only the sound that made it distinctive. The notes seemed more connected when she sang; there was an intuitive inner logic tying them together.

At the sound of her voice, Gottfried turned around—he was not the only one—and saw a face just as striking. Not conventionally beautiful, at least not in the sense he was used to. She was small and pale, with thick eyebrows, prominent cheekbones, and dark curly hair pulled back from her forehead, which was high and broad. Her eyes were black, the kind of black that made you look deep into them because it was hard to distinguish the iris from the pupil.

Someone told him that she was a pianist, which delighted him because he needed a sonata partner for a chamber music class. When she accepted his offer to work together, he was overjoyed, though he still had no idea how she played. In the conservatory everyone was sure to be pegged with a label very quickly, but she was a first-year student who, it seemed, had arrived only recently from somewhere in the East. No one knew her playing yet. In any case, her voice seemed to guarantee a natural musicality.

They started playing together a few days later; her piano tone had the same limpid clarity as her voice. She didn't have tremendous power, which was something of a problem, because they were working on a Brahms sonata. Her hands were too small and delicate for some of the stretches and awkward chord formations in Brahms' piano writing. She made plenty of mistakes, but they were both learning the piece for the first time. The mistakes were usually just wrong notes, yet they weren't clumsily played; it wasn't a question of faulty rhythm or a lack of responsiveness to the violin part. No, her rhythm was superb, he thought, and her sense of tempo much more instinctive than his. She never banged, even when she was groping for the notes, so her mistakes rarely sounded unmusical. Besides, he had enough to attend to in his own part of the sonata, and he wasn't a perfect player either.

It would have been hard for Gottfried to explain this, and perhaps he was never objective about Marietta, but the lightness of her tone never seemed superficial to him, not even in the Brahms D Minor Sonata. Maybe it wouldn't have projected to the last row of a large hall, but she would have drawn the audience into her orbit. There was a quiet, hidden power in this small woman; when she spoke to him in the school cafeteria, eliding the words in curious un-German patterns with her Romanian accent, people sitting nearby tended to stop their conversations and listen.

After working with her for a few weeks, he had to go on tour for a month as concertmaster of a chamber orchestra. This month seemed very long to him, but at least it was filled with work: in addition to the tour schedule, he had some important recitals to prepare for the coming spring. He decided to ask her to play them with him. But he didn't want to make the offer in a letter or on the telephone; he would wait till he got back to school and ask her in person. He could have been businesslike about the recitals in a telegram, but this collaboration meant more to him than a business arrangement, and he wanted it to mean more for her, too.

They were supposed to be just friends and colleagues, but he missed her so much that it scared him. During this month anything could happen. She might meet someone else; whatever feelings she had begun to have for him, if any, might evaporate.

He wasn't inexperienced with women. Every day on that tour he asked himself what had kept him from taking her hand in his, from telling her how he felt. But he knew the answer: sometimes women had accused him of rushing them, so this time he was afraid to push things too fast. The attraction between them should develop naturally, he had thought, and he hadn't found the right moment to talk to her about anything but music before he left.

The day he returned to Cologne, he had a few hours to kill before his rehearsal with Marietta. Too impatient and nervous to practice, he left the Hauptbahnhof and headed toward the

Old City. He needed to take his mind off the possibility that she might not share his feelings.

With renewed awe he gazed up at the spires of the Cathedral as he walked in its massive shadow. He stopped for a minute and began to feel the calm emanating from the majestic structure, the quiet but overwhelming authority of things that stand for centuries and do not change.

Suddenly a side door opened and three SA officers emerged, smartly dressed in crisp brown shirts. Planting their considerable bulk in front of each portal, they stood as firm and stalwart as tree trunks in a jarring modern counterpoint to the carved saints and prophets staring down from the gables.

What were they doing in the Dom? he thought. Surely they hadn't come there to pray—they would look to the Party for spiritual guidance. Did they still attend services out of habit, because they'd been brought up as good Catholics? No, it seemed more likely that they had been monitoring the sermon for any kind of subversive content.

Latter-day shepherds, he thought, watchful of their flock.

A thin stream of worshippers trickled past them. It was chilly: the men and women leaving the shelter of the Dom braced themselves against a gust of wind. The men pulled up the collars of their raincoats, clapped their hats onto their heads and drew the brims down toward their eyes. The women hurriedly buttoned their woolen overcoats as they passed the Brownshirts without looking at them. Yes, already an accepted fixture of daily life. Or were all those women simply too shy to look directly at such robust standard-bearers of German manhood?

Their high heels made a dry, clacking sound against the pavement as they hurried off toward homes and shops. Gottfried closed his eyes for a moment before continuing on his way. All around him, the footsteps of male and female church-goers combined in a percussive chorus that made him think of teeth chattering in the wind.

He was relieved when he got to the Altstadt, one of his fa-vorite haunts. He didn't want to think about the Brownshirts, not when he was going to see Marietta in a couple of hours. Most of the streets in the area were too narrow for cars and trams, so it was very quiet. Few people were out walking; it had just struck noon. Tourists were relaxing in cafés and restaurants. Shopkeepers were enjoying sandwiches and beer with their families in the back rooms of the shops. It gave him a childlike pleasure to imagine that he had this storybook part of the town to himself.

He strolled through the familiar winding streets down to the Rhine embankment and back up again, and even found a few charming cul-de-sacs and alleyways he'd never seen be-fore. He loved the feel of the cobblestones under his feet. The wind had died down, but it was still a cool, crisp autumn day. The sun highlighted the pinks and light blues and greens of the old houses. Outside each shop hung a wooden sign pro-claiming the trade practiced within.

After half an hour of pleasantly aimless wandering, he re-alized with a start that Marietta had been absent from his thoughts since he had reached the Altstadt. He had grown so accustomed to daydreaming about her whenever he had any time to himself—practicing, eating, strolling through the streets and parks of cities he'd visited on tour—that it seemed strange to become completely absorbed in something else. A sense of self-preservation made him feel good about this mo-mentary distraction, this proof that his emotions and enthusi-asms could occasionally wander.

He began to worry again about exactly how to propose the concert tour. The problem was, he couldn't picture her now without imagining his arms around her, his lips pressed against her neck, and he had decided that today he must let her know how he felt. He didn't know which to do first—offer to concertize together or tell her she meant more to him than just a recital partner.

He passed a newspaper stand where the *Völkischer Beobachter*—that upstart Nazi rag, as he had once called it—was displayed more prominently than the respectable *Kölner Stadt-Anzeiger*. Then, turning a corner, he found himself in front of the Goldener Adler. He hadn't been there since the unpleasant conversation with Ernst more than a year earlier.

He hesitated at the entrance to the café, but the familiar smells of roasted meats and potato pancakes drew him in. He'd had nothing to eat yet that day; during his train trip he had had no appetite. Suddenly he was quite hungry. As soon as he stepped in, he felt the warmth emanating from the kitchen and from plates steeped with hot food as waiters hurried past. The café was crowded; almost every table was taken, but he was lucky enough to find a small one in a corner, being cleared by a waiter. As he made his way toward it, zigzagging around tables and chairs, he picked up bits and pieces of several animated conversations.

He ordered chicken broth and potato pancakes with applesauce. He'd gotten slightly chilled outside and was shivering. After a few spoonfuls of soup, he began to feel warm inside and was grateful when he felt the warmth spread to his hands and feet. His fingers, which had been clenched around the handle of his violin case, began to loosen up. He wanted to play well at the rehearsal with Marietta; he was afraid that his nervousness about talking to her would spill over to his playing. It was one thing if his voice would shake; nobody expected him to be a polished speaker. But he couldn't afford to sound shaky on his instrument, not today.

He looked over at the table where he had sat with Ernst the last time, and began to notice the other diners. There was the usual assortment of university students, laborers, shopkeepers and old men dining alone at small tables. Only the old men and a few students were wearing ties; the students had loosened theirs. Despite the ambient noise, which would have sapped his concentration, some of those young men were leaning over books that lay open next to their plates; they seemed to be absorbed in study while they ate. At a few of the larger tables, the plates had been cleared away and card games were in progress. Clouds of cigarette and cigar smoke hovered in the air.

At the biggest table in the middle of the room, a dozen men were leaning forward, resting their chins or cheeks on their fists or between two outstretched fingers. They were listening attentively to one man at the far end of the table. Gottfried couldn't see him well from his seat, so while he was waiting for his potato pancakes, he walked over to get an idea of what the man was talking about. The crush of tables, chairs, waiters and customers was such that he had to get within a few feet of the speaker to be able to see him. And then he froze.

The object of everyone's attention was a thickset Bavarian in lederhosen and a green feather hat, which he hadn't bothered to take off for his lunch. His sleeves were rolled up, exposing enormous hairy forearms and pudgy hands, which jabbed the air in front of his bulbous nose whenever he made a point. But what jumped out at Gottfried was the swastika armband on each sleeve, just below the shoulder. His chair was pushed back from the table and he was standing, but he was so short and round that Gottfried hadn't noticed the man was on his feet until he was practically next to him. He even caught a drop or two of spittle as the fellow jacked up the pitch of his oratory.

It was the usual stuff: International conspiracies against Germany. The unfairness of Versailles. The inflation and food shortages of the twenties as well as the more recent Depression were all engineered by a cartel of banks in the hands of the Jews. He ranted about the Communists. And the need to rearm. To hell with the League of Nations and the treaties that tied our hands.

Only half-listening to the tirade, Gottfried stared at the swastika, that ancient symbol that the Nazis had appropriated and plastered all over the country. He thought of Ernst's pupil—a mere boy who probably didn't know the full implications of his party affiliation. But this middle-aged café demagogue seemed to know all the formulas and catchwords by rote, as if he'd mouthed them at street corners and in barrooms for years. A tried-and-true member of the New Order, and probably a veteran of a few street battles, too. Gottfried imagined those fat fingers curled around a club as the bully and his friends charged into a demonstration of socialists.

Gottfried turned away from him and scanned the group of listeners. Sailors, railway workers proud of their new Reichsbahn uniforms, housepainters with smears of white, gray and pink on their hands and faces and stray chips of plaster in their hair, all nodding their heads with enthusiasm whenever the speaker emphasized a point by pounding his fist on the table. Gottfried looked around at the other tables and found to his relief that this oaf hadn't yet reached a wider audience. The better-dressed, more educated clientele seemed to be ignoring him, but some nearby customers intent on enjoying a tranquil meal glanced over the tops of their newspapers at the speaker and shook their heads with irritation. Apparently he was aware of this; once in a while he aimed his oratory and his spittle in their direction. And then he noticed Gottfried.

"What are you staring at?"

"Nothing. I . . . I'm just waiting for them to bring my food."

"Are you with me or against me?"

"I . . ." Gottfried looked away, at his corner table, where the waiter had just deposited a plate of pancakes. "Excuse me, my food is ready."

"What's the matter, are you a Jew-lover?" He laughed, screwing up his beady eyes, which were almost lost in the fleshy folds of his cheeks. His admirers laughed with him.

"Or are you a Jew?" one of them added.

He remembered Ernst's words: *If I have any self-esteem, then I must be a Jew-lover.* But he didn't say that; he just backed off as the pig swilled down half a mug of beer, wiped the foam from his mustache with the back of his hand and proclaimed, "No, he can't be a Jew. Doesn't have the nose."

"But he walks like a Jew!" another one of them called out gleefully as Gottfried turned and started back toward his table. Out of the corner of his eye he saw the fellow rise halfway from his chair and imitate an apelike walk, to the intense amusement of his friends.

Back at his table, Gottfried looked without appetite at the pancakes, feeling his face redden. He slowly pulled a couple of bills from his wallet and placed them on the table. Then he picked up his violin and hurried out.

The day didn't seem so fine to him anymore. He wasn't in the mood for strolling or sightseeing. The Altstadt had lost its charm.

The Goldener Adler used to be like a second home to him. He'd had countless meals there, had played cards and chess and read the papers. But it had changed ownership recently;

he'd heard that somewhere and had forgotten it until this moment. Now the café harbored the likes of that bastard!

He had almost achieved the composure he needed for his meeting with Marietta and now it was shot to hell. He had read about party cadres like this in the papers but had never actually seen one in action. And his listeners! How could they buy that crap? With relief, Gottfried remembered the irritated faces of some of the other customers, and the rest who were ignoring him. "Still the majority," he muttered to himself as he rushed toward the Hochschule. "At least in this part of the country. This isn't Bavaria."

Now he couldn't wait to see Marietta. It didn't matter if he stammered, expressed himself awkwardly, played badly, made a fool of himself. It didn't even matter if she rejected him; he just needed to see a reasonable person—in fact, any students or teachers at the Hochschule would do right now, anyone who loved Bach and Mozart and Brahms. He turned the corner into the street where the Hochschule stood, and bounded up the stone steps that led to its massive entrance.

Above the portal were bas-reliefs of mythic figures with lyres and flutes. He'd never paid much attention to the serene faces of the Muses and other deities depicted there, but now he stopped in the middle of his flight up the stairs to look at them for a few moments. On a side panel Orpheus was shown playing to the beasts, which were tamed with wonder at his song. On the opposite panel he was descending to the underworld, soothing the tormented spirits of the dead with his lyre. At any other time these representations might have struck Gottfried as old-fashioned or pompous or sentimental, but now he didn't care. Their familiarity, combined with the rather naïve belief in the power of music that was projected by those scenes, was of some comfort to him.

Inside, he paused in front of the same bulletin board where Ernst's name had been crossed off the graduation program. He shuddered, didn't want to think anymore about their last conversation at the Goldener Adler. He headed toward the second floor, where most of the classrooms and practice studios were. On the way upstairs, everything that was familiar made him feel a bit safer: the broad, deep marble steps leading to the mezzanine, the dimly lit hallways where he had sometimes paced before jury examinations, the heavy double doors that insulated the studios.

As usual, strands of phrases—climactic moments from Beethoven or Schubert piano sonatas, Chopin preludes, Brahms intermezzos—filtered through to the corridor despite the thickness of walls and doors. At the far end of the second floor was the orchestra rehearsal hall. Yes—it was a Tuesday afternoon, they were rehearsing. He could make out the anxious strains of the opening of Mozart's Fortieth Symphony, mingled with the piano music coming from the studios nearby.

He slumped against a wall. His back slid slowly down the cool plaster, and he cradled the violin case against his chest. He crouched there for a moment, then with a soft thud his bottom hit the floor and he stretched out his legs.

Gottfried covered his eyes with one hand as they filled with tears. Fortunately, it was the middle of the hour: no one was in the corridor. He knew it would look strange to anyone who might walk by—a grown man sitting on the floor, like a child, with tears dripping down his cheeks.

––––––––––

"By now a dozen concerts have been lined up for the spring, and I'm being considered by Schmidt's management for next season."

"That's wonderful." Her face radiated goodwill toward him. Marietta seemed incapable of jealousy of someone else's success; she was too complete in herself. But he wanted to find something beyond friendliness in her face.

"I'd like you to play the recitals with me."

She blushed with pleasure and looked down at her hands, which were resting on the keyboard. But her expression changed suddenly, and the color drained from her face.

"There's going to be a problem," she said.

"Are you worried about the repertoire? I know there will be a lot, but you can take your time learning . . ."

"That's not it." Her eyes locked onto his almost fiercely. Suddenly he felt as if he had done something wrong. "Didn't you know I was Jewish?"

He hadn't known. She was foreign, exotic, but he'd never asked about her religion. She could just as well have been a Gypsy, for all he cared. He told her it made no difference to him, but she was adamant: A public collaboration wouldn't be a good idea. It would be risky for them both, she said—for him in his future career in Germany, and for her if or when she needed to get out.

Considering the scene he'd just witnessed in the Goldener Adler, it was hard to argue with her. Gottfried was too ashamed to tell her about the rabble-rouser and his crew, even though they had shaken him up so much that he needed to talk to someone about it. He hadn't stood up to them, and he didn't want Marietta to know that.

But surely the fact that most people in the café had been oblivious to the Nazi, and some even annoyed by him, was a good sign. He and the kind of people who listened to such talk were still the minority; Gottfried was convinced of that, even if they were gaining strength. In any case, lowlifes like the ones he'd just seen at the Goldener Adler had little to do with the concert world. People who loved great music couldn't be taken in by the gross oversimplifications that appealed to the uneducated.

"Look, there are still many Jewish artists performing in Germany. I admit, they're usually playing with each other, they play less and less with Aryans, but there's no law against it. At least not yet. Let me speak to a friend of mine who just started working at Schmidt's. Let's see what's still possible."

"Let it go," she said miserably. "It wasn't meant to be."

He said, only half-believing it, that this situation with the anti-Semitism in Germany couldn't last; there were enough people who didn't feel that way, and many who were completely against the Nazis.

"You mean you think the Nazis will be voted out?" she asked with a bitter smile.

He shrugged, as if to say there was no other way, feeling foolish because he knew there would be no more elections. Then he thought of something else. "Maybe if there's enough pressure on them from other countries, they'll ease up a little."

"You're more naïve than I thought," she said, her voice lower than he had ever heard it. Her smile turned into a grimace.

Everything between them until that moment had felt innocent; even his sexual attraction to her had felt as if it was elevated to an idealistic plane as pure and airy as her voice, and now she was speaking to him with tired contempt. What had he done? He'd wanted to offer her an opportunity that would advance her career, offer them both a way of working together continually, of sharing their love for music.

He looked away from her, and when he turned back he saw that the grimace had frozen as she struggled to fight back tears. He reached out to touch her shoulder. She shook her head vehemently, as if the tiniest disturbance would upset the tenuous balance that kept her from dissolving.

"Marietta . . ." His voice sounded different to him, thick with emotion even in those four quick syllables. He repeated her name and once again heard a voice that was no longer dry, commonplace, matter-of-fact. She looked at him, her lips slightly parted, her deep black eyes half closed.

"We can keep working together," he said, "at least in the class. I don't know if you felt the same way I did every time we played the slow movement of the Brahms sonata last month. Music never meant as much to me, I was never able to forget my own problems like that. I'm not quite sure how to tell you . . . but I'm so glad you came into my life."

A smile was struggling to break through the rigid cast of her face. Her eyes began to blink rapidly. As the tears came, he pulled her toward him.

———————

The next month was the happiest of his life, but by January 1935 she had to leave the Hochschule. The Nazi director who had been installed in the spring of '33 finally had his way over the objections of a number of professors and saw to it that no Jews remained in the school. Soon afterward Marietta told him she was moving to Frankfurt with her family. Her father worked for a Jewish organization there, which promoted all sorts of cultural events and helped Jews emigrate to other countries.

"We'll find a way to stay together," she said.

"How? You'll be leaving the country." The pleading, the despair he heard in his own voice frightened him. They had spent so much time with each other during that month, playing through a large part of the sonata repertoire, but also going to movies, plays and concerts. He could hardly imagine coming to the Hochschule every day without seeing her, without hearing that voice.

"One of the projects my father is organizing concerns Jewish musicians. Huberman and Toscanini want to form an orchestra in Palestine next year or the year after. As far as I know, the auditions are only for players with Jewish blood, but maybe . . ." She looked at him shyly. "Maybe they could make an exception where mixed marriages are concerned."

After she left, he couldn't concentrate on his work. His violin teacher, Professor Kerner, noticed the change in his playing and asked what was wrong. Gottfried had never confided in him before, but as he looked into the old man's watery gray eyes, he needed to unburden himself. As far as anti-Semitism was concerned, he knew he could trust him. Kerner was one of the teachers who had opposed the expulsion of Jewish students from the Hochschule, and he was the one who had fought for Ernst's right to play the Brahms Concerto.

His eyes widened as Gottfried told him of his love for Marietta. But when Gottfried spoke about her father and the plans for a Jewish orchestra in Palestine, Kerner rose from his chair and walked over to the window. "I've already heard something about this proposed orchestra," he said, gazing out at the street. "There will be so many displaced Jewish musicians that I doubt the orchestra will have room for non-Jews."

He turned back toward Gottfried, who could see the anxiety in his face.

"And frankly, if you decide to stay in Germany after all— for whatever reason—you could find yourself in an awkward position. Not so much because of your involvement with Marietta. That sort of thing is not uncommon, especially in the music world. But a connection to a Jewish organization like her father's could eventually be dangerous."

Gottfried told himself that the professor's fears were exaggerated. After all, didn't the government want the Jews out of Germany? One of the items on the agenda of her father's committee was emigration.

The next month he heard from Marietta that auditions for the new orchestra would soon be held in Frankfurt, and that with her father's help she had landed a job as staff accompanist for those auditions. This would enable her, she hoped, to ask for a favor, a double favor really—that Gottfried, a promising young soloist and a Gentile, could try out for one of the concertmaster positions rather than simply for the violin section. Competition for those seats was bound to be intense, because the Jews already had several of their own Kulturbund orchestras in Germany, and their concertmasters would need to emigrate sooner or later, probably to Palestine.

Another major obstacle remained: she would have to tell her parents about him and their hopes to marry. She had already told Gottfried that her father didn't take kindly to the idea of intermarriage, especially in such times as these. He was furious that Hitler had been elected chancellor, and constantly reproached himself for having made the mistake of moving to Germany with his family several years earlier. In Romania he had been a theater and opera director; in 1931 he was asked to direct *Salome* and *Elektra* in Cologne, then decided to settle there with his family, believing he would find more opportunities and greater artistic freedom than in his own country.

VIII

Late in the afternoon, a guard came to take him to the "concert hall." He wasn't the same one who had escorted Keller the first day, nor was he one of the guards who had been posted alongside the walls. They all looked even more alike to Keller than the prisoners. He hadn't paid much attention to them anyway, having seen their types in the Army dozens of times before: the jowly, overfed variety and the square-jawed strutting heroes, whose tight lips were always drawn into a thin line except when they were shouting orders. They looked at you, yet their steely eyes didn't let you in when you spoke; you could tell there was a moat between you and them even if you were only three feet apart. But Rudi (he told Keller his name within two minutes of walking together) was different.

His dark brown eyes were soft, almond-shaped, a bit puzzled-looking behind his glasses. His build was slight, there was no swagger in his walk, and even the gun he carried seemed less dangerous in his hands than it would in anyone else's; he held it loosely and it swung back and forth like a toy with his footsteps. His full lips were pursed most of the time, his brows drawn toward his eyes as if he were continually contemplating some philosophical problem just beyond his grasp.

Gottfried felt an immediate kinship with Rudi, especially when he began to ask some questions about Bach, but the young man's presence here disturbed him. He wished he'd met him years earlier, after a concert somewhere, in one of the cities that he visited while on tour. Or maybe in a park, or on the street—anywhere but in this place. He looked like a university student who'd been drafted, like almost everyone else who hadn't volunteered for the Wehrmacht. Somehow he had ended up here, in the SS. That meant it could have happened to anyone.

"You play a lot of Bach, don't you? For violin, by itself?"

Gottfried nodded, surprised that a guard would have any interest in what he played.

"I used to have a recording of the Chaconne." He smiled and shook his head. "The discs got scratched and finally wore out because I listened to them over and over. I couldn't believe a single violin would be able to do all that."

And Gottfried could hardly believe that a man wearing that uniform would have the curiosity or the passion it must take to listen to Bach's Chaconne so many times. Nothing in his experience with the wounded soldiers had prepared him for this.

"Tell me, what does it feel like when you play it?" Rudi asked.

"Well, it's a privilege, of course." Gottfried thought of some of the difficulties he'd had while practicing the piece recently, trying to get a pure sound in the chords despite the fatigue that would build up in his left hand. "And a challenge. Not always easy to live up to."

"The first few times I listened to that recording, I wondered if the violinist was improvising some of it—that stormy section, you know? It works up to such a huge climax, then parts of it are like a chorale, and other parts . . . well, almost like a sermon, but without words. It made me wish I could play an instrument."

"A sermon . . . I've never thought of it that way. You must be a churchgoer."

"Used to be," he said quickly. Gottfried wondered if church attendance was a sore subject for Rudi, as it had been for him.

"And a concertgoer," Gottfried suggested.

Rudi sniffed. "Not lately. Before the war, yes, when I had time—if I could afford a ticket."

As they walked on, Gottfried remembered arguing with his parents about whether or not music—in itself, without text—could provide a religious experience. At the age of eighteen he had invoked the Chaconne as an example of music's spiritual power when he stopped going to church every Sunday. They couldn't understand; they'd never been *inside* a piece like that, never felt their entire bodies galvanized by the massive sweep of those arpeggios, never held their breath in the hushed, hymnal phrases in D major just after the storm.

He wanted to learn more about Rudi, especially what could have caused him to join the SS. But there was no way to ask him about that directly, so he began with a simple question.

"From Leipzig," Rudi answered. "Bach's city."

Gottfried remembered the imposing statue of Bach, the Cantor of Leipzig, in the square next to the church where he labored for so many years. "Did you ever go to the Thomaskirche?"

"My family attended services there every Sunday. Once at Easter time—it must've been the year before the war started—we heard a performance of the *St. Matthew Passion* in the

Thomaskirche. I was sixteen then, and it made a huge impression on me, on the whole way I looked at religion and music. And the world."

"I can imagine. It's overwhelming music, and in that setting, with the spirit of Bach hovering in the air . . ."

"When I was home on leave a couple of years ago, I bought a recording of the *Passion,* which I've kept with me ever since." His voice dropped to a half-whisper. "I have it here, and a small turntable that I keep locked under my bunk. Not that there's any rule against simply having one."

"I suppose you don't want to draw their attention to it."

"No one would mind if I played the 'Horst Wessel Lied' or some of those dance tunes they like to listen to. Anyway, when the others are out, if I have a free hour, I play two or three of my Bach discs very softly."

"That's too bad. You can't possibly get the impact of the big choruses that way." Gottfried looked at the mud and ice underfoot, then at a row of blocklike huts just beyond the fence they were skirting. He wondered if he should hide his astonishment to be speaking with anyone here about that glorious music, whose message was so at odds with what surrounded them.

"It doesn't matter. It's enough to remind me of the way it sounded—and felt—in the Thomaskirche. And when the loudspeakers are blaring at roll call, if I'm not on duty, I go back to my barracks and listen at normal volume. I even bought a score to be able to follow the text while I listen, but it's frustrating because I can barely read the notes."

He paused for breath, but it seemed like something was still on his mind, some question he wanted to put to Gottfried. His eyes were fixed on the ground a few steps ahead of them, and he moved his lips once or twice as if he was about to speak. Maybe some of the music was running through his head and he was mouthing the words, Gottfried thought.

"Have you ever played it?" he finally asked.

"*St. Matthew*? Yes . . . years ago, in Cologne, I was concertmaster of the second orchestra for a few performances at the Gürzenich."

Rudi stopped walking for a moment and turned to look directly at Gottfried. "So you played the violin solo in the aria about Judas and the thirty silver pieces?" he asked breathlessly.

"Yes, I did. What's it called again? Oh, yes: 'Gebt mir meinen Jesum wieder.' " He remembered the rapid scales that evoke the sound of coins bouncing on the floor of the Temple when Judas throws them down. "But why are you so interested in that aria? It's not the most special one."

"The whole piece is overpowering, but—can you believe it?—for the past few months I haven't been able to get that little tune out of my head. It's so bouncy and lighthearted."

"It was fun to play, but I would have liked a chance with the other violin solo, the one in the 'Erbarme dich' aria."

"My question is, why did Bach write it that way? Judas is in despair, he's about to hang himself, and here we have an aria in G *major*. Not minor. No soul-searching, only tone-painting, the clink of those coins on the Temple floor. It's strange, coming so soon after the 'Erbarme dich.' Haunting, the lilt of *that* melody—some of the saddest music I've ever heard. But then, a few minutes later, a cheerful tune comes along, with miniature fireworks for the violin. I don't get it."

"I'm no expert on sacred music, but it must be for the sake of contrast."

"I don't think that's enough of a reason. You have to understand, it's only because I love Bach so much that this bothers me. I know I have no right to say this, but . . . he could have done better. Remember how the Evangelist tells of Peter's despair when the cock crows and he's just denied Christ for the third time? There's such pathos in the way Bach set those words. So why didn't he show the same kind of imagination when Judas is asking for his Jesus back, when he realizes the coins mean nothing to him?"

"I'm sure it's not a question of lack of imagination."

Gottfried had never given much thought to the psychological nuances of the various arias in the work. The musical vision in *St. Matthew* was so huge, so compelling, that he'd simply accepted the different keys, tempos and moods as a given. The story of Judas' betrayal had always made him uncomfortable; now he struggled to remember the details, to find an explanation of Bach's choices that would make sense to Rudi, and to himself.

"The difference must be that he wants us to identify with Peter, but not with Judas. The aria isn't sung from his point of view: we see him from the outside, so all we hear is the clink of coins."

Rudi tried to say something, but Gottfried continued, afraid he'd lose his train of thought. "We don't experience his longing to get Jesus back, we've only heard about that second-hand from the Evangelist. Anyway, by the time this aria comes along, I think Judas has *already* hanged himself. Yes, that's right—it's too late for him. He's 'the lost son,' throwing the blood money at our feet."

Rudi shook his head. "I still think it's an opportunity Bach missed. I mean, the man has just killed himself. Why make it so damned cheerful?"

"Remember, he wrote the *Passion* for a congregation, not a concert audience. It was a way for people to come together in worship. So I guess this aria is in a major key with that bouncy rhythm to show our detachment from Judas' treachery, to rejoice in *our* rejection of that money. It doesn't matter how he felt when he threw away those coins."

"Yes, Bach and his congregation could afford to detach themselves from Judas." Rudi grimaced. There was a bitter edge in his voice. "And from Pilate, too. But today . . . here"—with his gun barrel he made a vague gesture toward the fenced perimeter of the camp—"it's impossible."

Just then Gottfried noticed the same cluster of inmates he'd seen that morning, hoisting sacks and crates onto a railroad car. A couple of guards were poking them in the ribs with their truncheons, prodding them to work faster. Rudi grabbed his arm and hastily steered him around the corner of a warehouse.

"Judas knew he'd done wrong and tried to undo it," he whispered. "He tried to give the coins back, but the High Priests wouldn't take them."

His grip tightened above Gottfried's elbow, and they stood still for a few moments. Gottfried knew Rudi wanted more of an answer from him, but he could find nothing to say.

"He was just the pawn of larger forces."

Gottfried felt an impulse to look through a window again, but didn't dare.

"It's supposed to be a religion of forgiveness," Rudi added plaintively, as if it were up to Bach, or the man who had written the text he set, to determine what would happen to the soul of Christ's betrayer.

"Maybe there are some sins that can't be forgiven," Gottfried said at last.

Rudi bit his lip and let go of the violinist's arm. They walked on in silence. When they got to the hall, Gottfried could see that the prisoners were already inside. Rudi left him at the door, wishing him good luck even though his brow was furrowed and he was clearly still upset about Bach's portrayal of Judas. Gottfried wished he could have given him a more satisfying answer to his question.

———————

The first thing he noticed was that no guards lined the walls today. As he took his violin out of its case and tuned the strings, he wondered why.

Their withdrawal must have been the next step in the Kommandant's procedure. His performances had to seem different from everything else here in order to have their intended effect on the inmates. That must be the idea. Music had to be brought back into their lives, undiluted by the presence of guards.

It all seemed to have been worked out in advance. And his cooperation had simply been assumed; it didn't matter how he felt about it. Well, what if he only went through the motions and played just badly enough to sabotage the experiment?

One of his pegs slipped because the weather was so cold and dry; the E-string went down more than an octave. Keller took his time tuning it back up and adjusting the other strings, trying to sort out his thoughts.

The guards had been withdrawn from the room, but that didn't mean they weren't watching. Or listening somehow— though with their tin ears, conditioned by the fox-trots and tangos blasting from those loudspeakers, they probably couldn't tell the difference between Beethoven and a Strauss waltz. Or between a refined tone and a scratchy one, with wooden phrasing like Ernst's pupil. They'd never know if he was holding back.

The Kommandant couldn't hold him accountable if the experiment failed.

But Rudi had just revealed a finely tuned ear for the psychological complexities of Bach's sacred music, even if he had no formal musical education. He didn't fit in here, anyway. Keller wondered if Rudi had been planted in this camp to lure him into saying something he shouldn't. Or to judge his playing. Could he really be as sensitive—and as innocent—as he seemed?

Keller loosened the hair of his bow slightly, straightened his shoulders and took a deep breath before launching into the first piece. Maybe he should try to do his best, after all. Besides, if he played well enough for the experiment to succeed, whatever that meant, it could help these particular inmates. Not the ones in striped uniforms he'd seen at the Appellplatz that morning. No: he knew in his gut there was no hope for them. But for his listeners, the "chosen ones," perhaps it wasn't a meaningless exercise, like playing for the wounded soldiers. A lot might depend on these performances.

He began with the first solo sonata by Paul Hindemith, whose music was too progressive for the authorities. Hindemith had been condemned as a "Bolshevik" composer, and his music put on display as an example of "degenerate art." Its pungent harmonies, tonal ambiguities and often ironic stance—its complete lack of sentimentality—were all anathema to the Nazis.

Whenever Keller had practiced this piece, he put on a heavy mute and closed all the windows and doors in his apartment. Now he thought again of Herr Maier downstairs, wondering if the old fellow had heard him. After a moment he shrugged it off. A violin is not that loud, especially with a practice mute. And his musical ignorance was a further assurance;

no, Herr Maier couldn't be the reason he was here. He must have been recruited for this experiment simply because nobody else was available.

It felt wonderful now to forget about the mute and dig into the bold, sharply accented opening movement, to let himself be propelled by its strong rhythmic currents. Within the first few notes the stage is set: the thematic material spans two octaves, with outlined triads and fourths vying for supremacy in the atonal fabric. Rising and falling sequences abound; motivic fragments are confronted with their own mirror images.

Even though he'd been forced to work on Hindemith, Berg and Bartók in secret, he felt more at ease with modern music than with the first day's repertoire. It was the dissonance that freed him. If he played slightly out of tune, it wasn't as glaring, even to his own critical ears. And he could approach Hindemith without so much concern for beauty of tone, because the music had harder edges than Bach. His sound was stronger, more focused today, and he didn't feel hamstrung by a lot of technical problems.

His concentration on the music was complete except for one thing: he kept thinking that the audience's reaction would have to be different from the day before.

Maybe yesterday you thought I wasn't much. But listen to me today. If you don't respond now, at least I'll know it has nothing to do with my playing.

The wistful, lilting slow movement carried Keller through constantly shifting keys and colors, intensifying into thorny chords. An accelerando leads to a Presto that plummets from the highest to the lowest registers, where the music briefly regains its repose. Near the end of the movement, the recurrent lilting figure makes one last appearance, extending itself and expiring on the keynote it has found, a tentative resolution in D.

He began to feel the presence of women in the room. The day before, he hadn't been able to tell them apart from the men. Perhaps today was a little brighter, so he could make out their shapes better. They were interspersed with the men, as they must have been the first day. Though they were all emaciated, there was a suggestion of roundness or softness in some of the huddled forms.

Reveling in the chromatic language of the lyrical Intermezzo, he noticed that one of the women sitting near him had full breasts, which contrasted strangely with the boniness of her face and arms. She and a few others were looking straight at him, with what might have passed for concentrated attention anywhere else. Here it was impossible to guess what they thought or felt, but at least they weren't staring through him, as if he weren't there.

The woman's chest fascinated him with its rhythmic rise and fall. The Kommandant was right, damn him—he needed this audience, and not just to have them listen to his playing.

How long had it been, he thought, since these women had seen anyone like him? He wasn't beaten down like their men, terrorized like the inmates he'd seen at that morning's roll call, and he wasn't a gun-wielding guard. He felt their eyes on him, imagined them following the motions of his hands. What echoes of their past lives could his playing awaken in them?

As he continued the sonata, he began to imagine there was one woman in the group whom he had to meet. A strange sort of certainty took hold of him, a sense of familiarity, expectation. The woman he wanted or needed was somewhere in the back of the room, in the shadows—a presence, not yet a face.

At the end of the Hindemith, the applause sounded a bit more spontaneous than on the first day. The opening bars of the next piece, a Bach sonata, were already running through his mind as he bowed. He was trying to gauge the tempo and the attack of the first chord. But when he raised his violin to play, the door swung open. An inmate was dragged in and placed on a bench by two guards. Keller believed he recognized the man from the day before, but there was no way to be sure: all those cadaverous faces had looked so much alike.

As the guards left, one of them barked out an explanation. "He didn't want to come. He was hiding under his bed." The man stared at the floor, his long, narrow face set in an expressionless mold. But when he looked up at Keller for a moment, there seemed to be a glint of resentment in his eyes.

Anywhere else the incident might have been laughable, but not here. It made it so obvious to Keller that his listeners were in the room because they'd been forced to come. This man hated his playing, he decided, and would do anything to avoid hearing him. The poor bastard had been discovered and humiliated—if he was still capable of feeling humiliation over something like this.

Was he a musician, too? A violinist? Or had he been a critic for one of their newspapers before being sent here? Keller felt like the man could see through him, could hear what a struggle it was for him to play well.

The other inmates had no visible reaction to the latecomer, so he went on with the program as though nothing had happened. But it was hard to get involved with the music; in his mind's eye he kept seeing that wretched man hiding under the bed. He pictured him crouching in the dark, or stretched out immobile beneath the bedsprings. What had the man felt when the guards entered the room? The door opening, their footsteps approaching. Hiding in a place like this— for any reason—could probably get you killed. He was lucky this time, Keller thought. They just forced him to come to my concert.

He was playing the rhapsodic prelude of Bach's Sonata in G Minor, trying as always to produce full, rounded chords and flowing figurations between them. Sometimes he heard a dull moaning, which seemed to correspond vaguely to the shape of the music. And from the intermittent creaking of the benches, he guessed that some people must have been swaying gently in rhythm with his playing. He half-opened his eyes a few times to make sure. This was their first genuine response to him, far removed from yesterday's ritual of clapping on command.

The lean, muscular G minor fugue came next, with its concise staccato subject, obsessive repeated notes and insistent pedal tones. The intensity that Keller brought to this movement amplified the creaking and moaning. Then the gentle undulations of the Siciliana and the warmth of its B-flat major tonality afforded some relief from the angular textures of the fugue. But the moaning continued, which alarmed Keller because there was nothing sensual in it; it seemed to him that these noises revealed a world of pain that had little to do with the mellifluous music. The cascading arpeggios and propulsive sequences of the final Presto were better suited to the guttural counterpoint his playing had set in motion.

When he finished the Bach, the clapping began to sound like real applause. But as it died away, he heard the same voice that had challenged him the first day.

"We don't want you here." The voice was weak, but each word was pronounced clearly, with weary determination. "Go away."

It was getting dark, and he strained to see who had spoken. Was it the man they had dragged in? No one moved. Keller didn't say anything, wondering if he had really heard or had only imagined those words.

Then a woman's voice broke the silence. "No, that's not true. Stay with us . . . please stay." This voice was a bit hoarse, or dry, as if it hadn't been used for some time. He kept trying to hear the simple, clipped rhythms of those phrases after they had faded into silence.

His ears were ringing from all the practicing and playing he had done. He had planned to finish with the Bach, but couldn't stop now, not after what the man had said. He wasn't going to admit defeat so easily. And how could he ignore the woman's plea? So he began the Ballade by Ysaÿe, his thoughts racing far from the music.

He pictured that warehouse full of shoes, and the train chugging away from the camp. Was he too blind to see some horror coming, preoccupied as he was with the petty concerns of his violin-playing? Maybe he should listen to the man and get out today, while he still could. But then the Kommandant's threat about the Gestapo chipped away at his resolve. If he left before the experiment was over, that might be all the evidence they needed that he was a security risk.

During the Introduction of the Ysaÿe he began to feel disoriented, dizzy; waves of sound swelled up and receded, buffeting him as he groped for an answer. Then the Ballade theme sounded forth, passionate, defiantly virtuosic. The moaning started again, only louder now, punctuated by muffled sobs. The sobbing came from just one woman, and he was almost sure she was the one who had asked him to stay. But these sounds were out of tune with the music. They didn't belong to the world of Ysaÿe; the Ballade was an emotional piece, but it didn't express *that* kind of emotion. Yearning, passion, yes, but not desolation and despair!

How could he play with those sounds invading his ears? He had to get this over with and get out of that room. His fingers ached, his head was throbbing. He garbled some passages toward the end of the Ballade in his haste to finish, and cursed himself as he bowed. There was no more moaning after the applause, thank God. The sounds were only an accompaniment to the music—so far.

That evening, in the silence of his room, the thoughts that had been unleashed during the Ysaÿe kept swirling through his head. If he left himself open to that moaning, if he let that swaying and creaking mesmerize him, he might become . . . *like them.* Yes, he could already see himself in a gray sack, head shaved, eyes staring. Why not? The Kommandant could keep him there, behind barbed wire, a gray-clad raving witness with no one to listen.

But no, he wouldn't become one of them. He had certain rights, after all. It was not for nothing that he had this room to himself, that in the concert hall they were a blurred mass in the shadows and he, removed from them by a few paces, received whatever light was to be had in that dark world.

He would keep himself separate.

But the woman's voice kept coming back to him: *Please stay with us.* He had to find that woman and talk to her.

Occasionally he heard footsteps not far from his window. A guard must have been pacing the perimeter of the camp. As the footsteps receded, everything grew quiet; in the stillness he could hear his heartbeat resounding in his skull, and there was a ringing in his ears like the hiss of steam escaping from a boiler, a piercing din that kept him awake half the night.

IX

"Thank you for agreeing to see me, Herr Lupescu."

"You said you were a friend of my daughter's?"

"We worked together in a sonata class at the Hochschule. I'm a violinist."

"Oh, yes—I think she told me something about you when you started playing together in the fall. She said you were quite talented. So, what can I do for you?"

His voice, a velvety baritone, seemed to create its own resonance in the thickly carpeted room. The walls of his study were lined with books, many of which were laid on their sides and stacked in order to maximize the space on each shelf. There were titles in Russian, French and German. Kleist's *Michael Kohlhaas* caught Gottfried's eye, as well as a worn copy of Büchner's *Woyzeck* with several bookmarks curling over the tops of the pages. On one shelf stood a few thick volumes with silver Hebrew lettering incised on the spines; he could almost feel the creamy softness of their leather bindings.

"Marietta told me something about the organization of Jewish artists you work for."

The bushy brows came together over Herr Lupescu's deep-set black eyes as he leaned forward and folded his soft white hands on the desk. He had a high forehead topped with wisps of grizzled hair, but on the sides his hair was as thick and curly as Marietta's. A gray cardigan fit loosely around his sloping shoulders.

"I have to admit, I'm surprised she would discuss it with someone who's not . . . in our circle."

"I believe she trusts me, sir. And she's proud of the work you do."

He made no response, but the full lips Gottfried had noticed moments earlier were now compressed. Gottfried cleared his throat, beginning to regret that he had come. Marietta had warned him about her father.

"I had an idea for a concert that she and I could play together, to raise funds to assist the Kulturbund in its work."

"Have you talked about this with her?" Lupescu's voice suddenly seemed tense, guarded; the words came out in a clipped monotone.

"No, it's a new idea I've had, since she left the Hochschule. You see, Herr Lupescu, I've signed with a management recently. I had wanted to make Marietta my accompanist, but she felt it wouldn't be a good idea, given the political situation."

He sniffed. "That's something of an understatement."

"I . . . I couldn't disagree, and was happy to continue working with her just in the class. Then, after she left, my manager suggested that I play a few house concerts for some wealthy people in Cologne and Frankfurt, in order to raise money to buy an old Italian violin. Also to make contacts that would be helpful in building my career. But I've decided it would be much more meaningful to play a concert to benefit the important work you're doing."

When Gottfried paused for breath, Herr Lupescu said nothing. His coal-black eyes, which at first had seemed friendly or at least civil, focused tightly in a visible effort to assess his visitor and figure out what he had really come for.

"A number of the potential donors mentioned by my management are Jewish," Gottfried added, feeling almost as if he should apologize to Marietta's father for making what had seemed like a generous offer before he met him.

"Then they probably contribute to us already," Lupescu said drily. "Excuse me, but I need to ask you something. In the last month that Marietta studied at the Hochschule before she was forced to leave, she spent a lot of time away from home. She said she had made some new friends with whom she was going to the theater, opera and so forth. When I asked if those friends were Jewish, she wouldn't give me a clear answer. I know her well enough not to press her when she doesn't wish to talk about something."

He paused, his beady eyes boring into Gottfried's as if he already knew the answer to the question he was about to ask.

"Were you one of the people with whom she was going out so often?"

"Marietta and I . . . were on very friendly terms."

"I see. Please understand: in principle, I have nothing against her making Gentile friends. She had several before we left Romania. You know, I used to run a theater in Bucharest. Jews, Gentiles—we all worked together. Assimilation . . ." A momentary grimace twisted his features. "The word never even crossed my mind. I only became aware of that word here, in the past few years, as a definition of what is no longer possible."

"I understand that you feel that way, Herr Lupescu, but . . ."

"Coming back to your offer, one thing you may have overlooked in your calculations was Jewish pride."

Why did he use the word "calculations"? Gottfried wondered.

"We could always use more money," he continued, "but we're not desperate, and until we are, I would prefer not to look beyond the Jewish community for help. Besides, money isn't our main problem. Getting visas from foreign consulates, smoothing things over with the Propaganda Ministry in Berlin—those are the tough things for us."

"Excuse me, sir, but it seems to me that promoting an insular attitude within the Jewish community would be giving the authorities what they want, playing into their hands."

"That's what we have to do in order to survive in this country." His voice was accusatory, as if his visitor had caused or somehow contributed to the problem. "And I don't think it's your place to say how we Jews should deal with the situation your country has put us in."

Gottfried's throat tightened. "Surely you don't believe that I support these new laws."

Maybe Lupescu realized he'd gone too far. He both acknowledged and brushed aside the young man's disclaimer with a perfunctory wave of a hand, shaking his head briefly, his lips forming a silent "No."

"I must confess I'm disappointed, Herr Lupescu. I thought that for a Gentile and a Jew to play together, even if only in a private concert, would be a gesture of solidarity."

"In normal times such a gesture of solidarity, as you call it, might mean something, but not now. The concerts and exhibitions we organize go beyond gestures. We need to insure our survival, culturally and, yes, physically: I'm sure the day isn't far off when that will be at stake, too. I'm sorry to disappoint you. You've made a . . . a generous offer, but it's simply not feasible at this time. I could say things might get better and we could use your help in the future, but I don't see much hope on the horizon."

He stood up; so did Gottfried. As Lupescu moved around the desk and toward the door, he added, "To be honest, young man, I'm not sure whether your disappointment is more for your idea of what would benefit us—or for yourself." The last few words came out very softly; he hadn't turned to face him.

Gottfried could think of nothing to say as the blood pumped into his cheeks. How could Marietta have grown up in the same household as this proud, bitter man? She would be furious with him for having had the clumsy audacity to approach her father with this grand idea.

Herr Lupescu opened the door, and Gottfried walked ahead of him through the narrow hallway to the front door of the apartment, where he half-turned to go through the motions of saying goodbye.

"I see now that it was a mistake to come here. Could I ask you not to tell Marietta about my visit?"

Lupescu hesitated, then nodded slowly. "In return I'd like you to consider that Marietta will leave for Palestine within the next few months. Please don't do anything that would deflect her from that purpose, from her safe destination. She must not be confused now."

Gottfried wanted to argue that her happiness was also at stake, but the proprietary expression in her father's eyes kept him from saying anything further.

———

"I had to see you."

She came in, pushed past him, tossed her coat onto a chair. She had never been to his apartment before, and this was not the way he had imagined her crossing the threshold for the first time. He wondered what she was doing back in Cologne. Had her father broken his promise and told her he'd come to see him last week? Or had the Gestapo raided the offices of his organization?

For the past few days he'd been haunted by the feeling that something would go wrong with their plans. Every hour was tinged with nagging doubts that interfered with his work and his sleep. Just before Marietta knocked at the door, he had been thinking that if the audition were scheduled for that day instead of the following week, he would never be accepted into the Palestine orchestra.

He wanted to ask her what had happened, but when they faced each other, he dropped his eyes. How could he hide from her what he had done? Or how could he find a way to tell her, if she didn't already know?

"I told my parents about you." Her voice was lower than usual, husky: she had been crying. "It was time. I couldn't keep up the sham any longer, not with the audition coming." She looked away, her jaw working, her eyes fixed on the opposite wall. "My father . . ."

She paused, swallowed. Even when she was upset, the way she held herself was striking. Her whole body, in its momentary immobility, was brimming with energy, and her stance was as centered as a ballerina's. Despite the plainness of her brown woolen suit, the mass of dark curls framing the pallor of her face made her look like a *maja* from an old Spanish painting—a figure poised on the brink of action, an image made real.

"My father threatened to disown me if I don't break it off."

This was no surprise to Gottfried after his disastrous meeting with him. And considering the political and racial climate in the country—every week a new restriction on what the Jews could do, every day more posturing and bullying in the streets—he couldn't entirely blame the man, even though he'd treated him with contempt. In the week since Gottfried had seen him, with his practicing going so badly, he had come to feel as if he deserved her father's scorn.

But she was looking at him again, and there was so much pain in her eyes that he felt he should be outraged by her father's threat. Never mind how Lupescu had treated *him*. In his bitterness over what was happening in Germany, and in the name of protecting her, he had trampled on his own daughter's happiness.

"It's worse than you expected . . ." Half question, half statement. Why couldn't he respond more forcefully? This was Marietta, his Marietta slowly nodding her head, not a figure from a painting—there was no frame, no two-dimensional canvas interposing itself like a screen between them. "What are you going to do?" Passive. He had no suggestion. He would let her decide.

"What can I do? I have to ignore what he said. Get around him."

"How do you mean?"

"He threatened to speak to the audition jury, to try to impose a rule that the orchestra be absolutely closed to those who aren't at least half-Jewish. The jury hasn't made up its mind yet; maybe a Jewish grandparent will be considered enough, but my father might have the power to influence the way things go."

"So how do we get around him?"

"By giving you some Jewish blood." There was a calculating glint in her eyes, those liquid deep black eyes now hardened with determination. "Through the Kulturbund I met a man who's very good at arranging papers. For a price, of course."

He remembered Professor Kerner's concern about the path he was on with Marietta. What if this didn't work and he was stuck in Germany and from now on, somewhere, there was a document attesting to his Jewish ancestry?

He was seized by a sudden impulse to cover her mouth, to do something that would block the steamroller of her will. It took an effort to keep his hands at his sides. He dropped his eyes, attempting to swallow the bitter saliva that was flooding his mouth.

She's just trying to find a way for us to stay together. Why am I clenching my fists?

Was it because she was more forceful and decisive in pursuing her plans than he could ever hope to be? Or was it because she was trying to turn him into a Jew?

"What's wrong?" she asked.

Until that moment, he'd never felt anything but tenderness toward Marietta. And since the day he returned from the chamber orchestra tour, there had been no need to disguise what was going through his head. Now he had to look up, keep the conversation going, respond somehow to what she had said.

"Nothing," he lied. "But speaking of blood, I doubt that my own parents would approve of your idea."

"Your parents? You've barely said a word about them." Was there a note of challenge in her voice, as if his parents, too, might thwart her plans? Or was she simply distracted? Just then it struck him that the whole focus of their relationship, by unspoken consent, had been Marietta and her need to emigrate, and their strategy for staying together. His background and his feelings about the future hadn't seemed that important; even his ambitions hadn't played much of a role.

"It's true I'm not very close to them," he admitted. "They

could never understand my wanting to become a musician. They thought it meant a bohemian lifestyle. Which it does, compared to the way they live. And now . . . it turns out that we don't see eye-to-eye politically."

She was watching him closely, and as he mentioned politics her eyes hardened again, in an inquisitorial stare.

"It's just that in spite of our differences, I love them, and the idea of never seeing them again . . . well, it's uncomfortable."

She said nothing, and there was no sign of comprehension in her face.

"More than uncomfortable. It's painful. That's all. I just had to say it, had to tell you. It doesn't mean I'm changing my mind. I'm just not used to . . . staring at the rest of my life and saying, 'This is the way it's going to be.' "

"We have no choice," she said softly. "Not if we want to stay together."

"I know." Finally able to unclench his fingers, he turned away and looked at his violin, lying in its open case on the table. "I just wish my practicing were going better. All these secret plans are making me nervous, making it hard for me to concentrate. I don't think I'll have the Beethoven Concerto ready for the audition next week. And now, knowing that your father's going to campaign against me makes it even harder. What if they don't take me?"

"Don't be silly. You're a wonderful violinist. You know, some of the players I accompanied last week have already been accepted. They were good, but no one's been on your level yet."

"They were accepted into the section. Concertmaster is different, especially in this situation."

"Yes, but you can do it. Listen . . . somehow you've got to learn to have more confidence in yourself. Not only in your playing, but in your decisions. Otherwise you'll never get what you want, even if you don't come to Palestine. Even if I weren't in your life."

She grabbed him by the shoulders, as if to shake him up, and stood at arm's length, studying him. Once again he dropped his eyes, embarrassed by her scrutiny. Until that day, she must have thought he was a decisive man, courageous to want to get involved with a Jew, not a doubt-riddled weakling who needed his parents' approval. It was true: he'd hardly ever mentioned them, because they weren't a big part of his life anymore. He didn't really crave their approval, but it was easier to talk about them than to say he had mixed feelings about leaving Germany with her.

He had shown her a part of himself she hadn't seen before. Would she think less of him, despise him?

He looked up and was relieved to find no judgment, no contempt in her eyes, only the need to know him better. At that moment he wondered how she could still love him. But she had to understand—Palestine meant uprooting himself. For her it was different; she was already uprooted.

"I guess it doesn't matter if they don't take me," he heard himself saying. "I could still try to get a visa and come to Palestine. Maybe find something else to do."

His voice sounded hollow, but she didn't seem to notice; the puzzled expression on her face gave way to a look of joy and loving triumph. She put her arms around his neck.

"You know, for a long time I've been obsessed with the Nazis, with all the restrictions they've forced on us. Every day I think about the persecution of my people and how it's probably going to get a lot worse. But now it turns out that the biggest obstacle to my freedom comes from the narrow-mindedness of my own father."

Gottfried remembered the rigidity that had come over her father's face as he tried to reach out to him.

"I can understand how he feels, though." It was hard to pretend he didn't know him. "Maybe, with time . . ."

"We don't have that kind of time." She shook her head emphatically. "Even though I love him, I'm not going to let him take away what I want most, even if he disowns me. You say all these secret plans make you anxious. You're worrying about your parents. What about me? Think of the pain I'll cause my father, and my mother, too, caught in the middle. I know she sympathizes with me, but she's not strong enough to stand up to him. They're both expecting me to cave in, and they're in for a big shock. Don't you think that weighs on me?"

Her eyes probed his, and he felt ashamed of his weakness.

"But if there's one thing these Nazis have taught me, it's to make sure that no one else runs my life. And that's why I came to you today." She looked briefly around his room. Her eyes rested for a moment on the bed in the corner. "I want to marry you. Now."

He could find nothing to say. He had been so careful not to rush things that her eagerness took him by surprise. And he didn't think this was the right time—not when he'd wanted to gag her just a few minutes earlier. How could he be sure he wouldn't feel that urge again, or something worse, when she was naked and defenseless in his bed?

She laughed for a moment, her shoulders hunching up in a nervous shrug. "Not officially. We can take care of that later, in Palestine." She pulled him toward her. "But what I've learned from playing sonatas with you is that the deepest musical experiences can happen in a room as well as on the concert stage. It doesn't matter what the world recognizes."

X

The third morning, Keller reached drowsily for his wristwatch on the chair next to the bed. He was surprised to see that it was already nine o'clock: he must have slept through the roll call! How was it possible with that loud music?

He lay in bed awhile, staring through the window. From that angle he couldn't see any barracks or fences. Or the Appellplatz, thank God. Just a gray patch of sky, framed by jagged lines of paint peeling off the walls and a rickety desk in front of the window. For a few moments he managed to pretend that everything in his field of vision was part of a painting—an interior scene with the window as both a source of light and the merest hint of a world outside—and tried to cloak this spartan "guest room" in an imaginary aura of rustic simplicity.

It seems that you don't approve of the camp.

He hated the idea of being the Kommandant's pawn, but he had no other choice; the bastard had made that clear enough. Besides, whatever might happen to his audience after

the experiment couldn't be any worse than what would happen to them if he weren't there. So once again he told himself
that he might as well do what the man wanted, and do it as
well as he could.

The fingers of his left hand were tapping against his chest
and stomach. He recognized familiar patterns from the pieces
he planned to play that afternoon.

He got out of bed, opened the door and brought in his
breakfast tray. He ate quickly and started practicing without
the usual procrastination. For the first time since his student
days, he was eager for a concert to begin rather than impatient
to get it over with. Something felt different in the actual playing, too. His fingers were moving more lightly; he worked
through problems more efficiently, brought difficult passages
to a satisfactory level with fewer repetitions.

Somehow his attitude had changed during the few hours
he'd slept. Maybe it was because of the memories that had
flooded him in the stillness of the night. It was the first time in
years he had allowed himself to remember Marietta without
forcing his thoughts in a different direction, the first time he
could picture her face.

If things had turned out differently, she might have been
in that room where he played each day, listening to him along
with the others through a filter of memories and hopelessness.
Thank God she'd gotten out.

If I had gone with her, I wouldn't be here either, he
thought. But he hadn't taken that chance.

Now nothing was left in his life but music. He needed to
regain some faith in himself as a performer, needed to break
down whatever barriers stood between him and his audience.
He knew now that if he wanted to reach the prisoners, he'd

have to be ready for any reaction from them—moaning, sobbing, or worse.

———————

That afternoon, he was disappointed when Rudi didn't come for him; he had wanted to talk some more about Bach with him. The prospect of being able to speak to someone who would actually listen, someone who might share the renewed enthusiasm he suddenly felt for music, had filled him with a kind of joy—if one could ever feel joy in such a place. He walked in silence next to the guard who had come for him.

He began the program with a sonata he had composed himself. It was his first performance of the piece, which would have been too dissonant to appeal to the wounded soldiers. He had no pretensions as a composer, and never would have attempted to play it at an important concert. Besides, in the last few years it would have been risky to present this work in public—it would have been condemned as degenerate. But here there were no printed programs, no music critics, no censors. Here, strangely enough, it seemed possible to offer this sonata full of anguish, whether or not it had any lasting value, as a personal response to the despair that surrounded him.

Inspired by Hindemith and Bartók, he had written the piece in a free atonal style. The manuscript, like his diary, was always locked in his desk drawer, but he knew it by heart. Two contrasting themes were derived from the same motivic roots, a few distinctive melodic intervals and rhythmic patterns embedded in the texture of each theme. Later, the two ideas were combined—played together in double-stops—and only then did their common motive begin to be audible. Gradually the two themes became one. But they didn't survive their union:

they disintegrated. Only the motivic fragments remained, and they, too, were broken down to their component parts—the individual notes, reiterated like low grunts or high-pitched shrieks. The first theme was supposed to sound strong, noble; the second, tender and beautiful. All that remained of them by the end was an impotent sputtering and a few protracted wails.

After he had been playing for a few minutes, the moaning began again. Getting louder, it might have disturbed him in any other piece, but it harmonized with his music. A woman started sobbing, and unlike what he'd heard the day before, these cries were no longer suppressed. Soon she was joined by two or three others. He heard groans from the men. Then, straining against its weakness, the cracked voice that had plagued him the first two days was raised once more.

"He shouldn't be here. Don't let him do this." The voice turned into a plaintive whine as it lost its battle against the rising tide of sound. "Stop him!"

The benches creaked louder and louder. The swaying grew furious in response to the death rattle of the themes of his sonata. Borne along by the waves of sound, he felt an unexpected kinship with those sufferers. They were united through this music of disintegration and despair—united against the oppressors, against the whole world outside that dark room.

As his piece ended, the sounds continued. Unwilling to lose momentum, he closed his eyes and plunged into Bach's Sonata in A Minor. How different it was from the way he had begun the sonata in the past, trying to hear the first few measures in his head before starting, attempting to capture the right tempo, the silence weighing heavily upon him. This time he didn't even try to convey the stately nobility of the prelude.

He knew he was diverting the music from its true course, twisting it to serve his purpose of the moment, but he didn't care. A few minutes later the fugue began, and it was no longer rational discourse, an elaboration of subject and countersubject among three voices. The springy, octave-vaulting motive jabbed the air and carried him forward through a labyrinth of keys, goading him into taking more and more risks. He had no idea how it sounded—there was too much noise to tell. But he knew that for the first time in his life, he was playing Bach with total abandon.

In the middle of the fugue, he opened his eyes to take in what was happening around him. Some of the inmates had backed into the corners of the room and were huddled together. It was the first time he had seen any of them touch one another. Three or four women crossed their arms and held themselves tight as they swayed, as though they were rocking babies. Some of the men tried to put their arms around them, to enter into their self-embrace, but the women seemed locked in private grief.

The children they lost.

Two men grabbed each other's shoulders. One stroked the other's face, which was streaked with tears. A man who looked even more skeletal than the rest of them broke away from the group and ran against a wall, hitting it again and again with his fists until his knees buckled and he collapsed. The uproar was something like that ringing in Keller's ears, the web of noise that often tormented him in the silence of the night. Only it was a hundred times louder, as if he and his violin were merely the sounding board of a much larger instrument—the whole building, vibrating with grief.

The prisoners were no longer in their seats. As they groped their way around the room, a few came very close to him, got in the way of his bowing. During the third movement of the Bach, an exquisite duet between a sinuous melody and a pulsing ostinato, his old frustration came back. He couldn't hear himself, couldn't concentrate; it was like trying to whisper by a waterfall. The serenity of the duet eluded him once again.

What makes you think your life will be different after this? What makes you think you'll play better? You're just the Kommandant's pawn, not a great artist. This is the power he offered you, and it won't last. It exists only here.

They started to touch him, but somehow he managed to keep playing. Bony fingers clung to his ankles. Desiccated breasts brushed against his arms. There was a bitter taste in his mouth; his tongue felt glued to his palate. Sweat was dripping into his eyes, trickling down his nose and cheeks.

He began the last movement of the Bach with a sort of relief. It was fast and fiery, more attuned to the clamor—a way of staving them off. He closed his eyes.

Just get to the end of the piece.

But when he got there, he couldn't stop. He began to improvise. He played as if possessed, as if he meant to break the instrument. It seemed like the only way to keep those people from tearing him apart. Strange chords, wild arpeggios, eerie glissandi burst from the violin. The hands were still on him, beseeching, provoking him, pulling the shirt off his back.

Finally he stopped playing, but the hands didn't stop. They kept jostling him, pushing, grabbing. He had to hold the violin high above his head to keep it from getting crushed. Then he lost his balance, almost fell.

"Stop it!" he screamed. "Get away from me!"

Fingernails dug into his cheeks and the back of his neck. The pain in his shoulders grew unbearable as he twisted and strained to protect his instrument. But suddenly the hands and bodies pulled away from him. Staggering toward a wall, he saw eight or ten guards rushing through the door. As he struggled to regain his breath, they pounced on the prisoners and started to beat them with clubs and gun butts.

Benches were knocked over. One was kicked against the wall near where he was standing, barely missing his violin. Though no one fought back, most of the inmates brought their arms up to shield their heads. He was afraid that would be enough provocation for the guards to start shooting.

He backed away to an empty corner. The room was filled with screaming, grunts, curses from the guards, the sickening thud of wood and metal smacking those bony shoulders and shaven heads.

Suddenly the Kommandant appeared, shouting, demanding order. The guards snapped to attention, their truncheons and guns at their sides. The prisoners quickly stifled their moaning. Keller stood there, frozen, barely ready to believe he was safe again. The room ached with the sudden silence.

———

Rudi caught up with him as he rushed back toward his room.

"Are you all right?"

Gottfried wasn't sure if the urgency in his voice came from breathlessness or from concern.

"I'm not hurt, just shaken up."

"I can imagine. Those people were about to tear you to pieces."

Maybe it was the worried look on his face that made Gottfried feel like he could trust him. Or maybe it was his desperate need the day before to know why Bach had abandoned Judas in his final moments.

"I don't think they were trying to hurt me. I meant I was

shaken up because of the way the guards reacted—with such force."

He didn't add that he felt responsible. He should have seen where the hysteria was leading. But what could he have done differently?

"You haven't been here very long." Rudi still sounded out of breath, as if he was struggling to keep up with Gottfried. "By their standards, I would say it was rather restrained."

But Rudi hadn't been in that room. How did he know so soon what had happened?

"Where were you?"

"Outside. Looking through a window."

Suddenly the obscenity of it struck him: the Kommandant and his henchmen peering at him and his audience of Jews as if they were laboratory animals in a cage, rescuing him just in time so he could still be used in the final phase of the experiment.

He stopped and turned to face Rudi. "Is that all you do around here? Just watch things happen?"

The doelike eyes narrowed; his lips parted as though he wanted to say something to defend himself but couldn't find the words. His jaw was quivering slightly.

"I'm sorry," Gottfried muttered. "I didn't mean that the way it came out. It's just that you're not like the other guards here. You're more . . . more like me, damn it. I don't understand what you're doing here, how you can go on from day to day."

"Oh, I manage." There was an edge of sarcasm in his voice.

"What those people must have suffered—they and all the others . . ."

"Don't think about their suffering. It'll make you go crazy, because there's nothing you can do to change it. Nothing any-

SHOREWOOD
PUBLIC LIBRARY

Visit the library's website at
www.shorewoodlibrary.org

Checked out item summary for
VAN WINKLE MARY B
06-25-2013 3:28PM

BARCODE: 35250001427525
LOCATION: 89am
TITLE: Creole belle : a Dave Robicheaux
DUE DATE: 07-16-2013

BARCODE: 35250001456854
LOCATION: 89am
TITLE: The prodigal son : a Carmine Delm
DUE DATE: 07-02-2013

BARCODE: 35250009972455
LOCATION: 89af
TITLE: The savior : a novel / Eugene Dru
DUE DATE: 07-16-2013

BARCODE: 35250001503077
LOCATION: 89anf
TITLE: Unsinkable : a memoir / Debbie Re
DUE DATE: 07-16-2013

DUE DATE 07-16-2013
TITLE Unsinkable : a memoir / Debbie Re
LOCATION 889M
BARCODE 32520041203011

DUE DATE 07-16-2013
TITLE The salon : a novel / Renata Hill
LOCATION 889M
BARCODE 32520000817455

DUE DATE 07-02-2013
TITLE The prodigal son : a Carmine Delm
LOCATION 889W
BARCODE 32520041202594

DUE DATE 07-16-2013
TITLE Creole belle : a Dave Robicheaux
LOCATION 889W
BARCODE 32520041452757

06-25-2013 3 28PM
VAN WINKLE MARY B
Checked out item summary for

www.shorewoodlibrary.org
Visit the library's website at

SHOREWOOD
PUBLIC LIBRARY

one can do. But let me answer your question: yes, as often as I can, I just watch things happen. I try not to participate, also not to look for answers." Suddenly his eyes seemed to lose their focus. "But sometimes the others watch me and wait, and I have to pull a trigger."

"My God, Rudi. How can you . . ."

"It's not as if they give you a choice, you know. The first time was horrible. I couldn't eat for two days. The worst part was, I couldn't let them see I was upset. The second time, a few weeks later, was a bit less sickening. By the third time, there was . . . no longer such a big line to cross."

Gottfried shook his head. "I wouldn't want to be in your shoes."

Rudi looked at him for a few moments, then laughed. It was a raucous, ugly laugh, surprising from someone so soft-spoken and gentle.

"Your shoes and mine aren't that different. Look, I'm just trying to survive until this fucking war is over so I can become human again. You know what I've discovered here, in this university of hell? A new moral law. If you're forced to commit a crime that would be committed without you anyway, and by resisting you would risk your own life, then it's no longer a crime. As long as you don't enjoy it."

"I'm not so sure about that."

"Yeah, sure, it's easy for you to say, with a violin in your hands instead of a gun. But don't cling too tightly to your beautiful world of music. It won't protect you from everything."

He caught Gottfried's arm and pointed to a lone, bent figure hobbling around near the back fence of the camp. "Do you know who that is? Do you know what he does here?"

Gottfried shook his head, straining to see the man in the

distance. It was getting dark; he could see him only in silhou-
ette. He was carrying a long stick in one hand.

"Is that a broom he's carrying?" he asked. "Is he some sort
of janitor?"

Rudi shook his head with a grim smile. "Well, I guess you
could say he's responsible for cleaning up. They call him—"

"Rudi!" A hefty, ruddy-cheeked Oberscharführer was glaring at them from across the internal barbed-wire fence. His
jowly face was already familiar to Gottfried from the "concert
hall," especially from a few minutes ago, when he had seen him
beating prisoners with gusto. "The Kommandant wants to see
you at once."

Rudi let go of Gottfried's arm and dropped his hand to his
side, moving quickly away from him. "Excuse me," he stammered. "I have to go." He disappeared with the other guard as
suddenly as he had come, and the violinist was left alone,
heading toward his room.

What was there between Rudi and the Kommandant? He
had sounded worried, as if caught on the verge of some major
indiscretion.

Gottfried kept looking for that bent man, craning his neck
for a better view of him, but he had vanished behind the win-
dowless building with the chimneys.

XI

He eagerly opened the thick envelope that had arrived from England. There were several sheets inside, which led him to hope for something more substantial than the perfunctory progress reports he had already received. The firm, bold handwriting was familiar, but it sloped in uncharacteristically jagged lines across the pages.

London, 3 March 1935

Dear Gottfried,

I've meant to write you for a long time. Not another summary of how things are going for me in my professional life over here—you've already heard about that, and I'm sure you know as well as I do that something was missing from those letters. No: I wanted to be as open as I could with you about our last meal together at the Goldener Adler. I feel I owe you an explanation.

In my eagerness to prove I was as much a German as the rest of you, I may have given you the wrong impression: it probably seemed like I was blaming you for what was happening all around us, like I felt superior to you. But I don't believe that. No, Gottfried, I'm neither better nor worse than you. The problem is, that's not good enough, and that's why I had to leave.

Let me explain. Do you remember Siegfried Bremer? He graduated from the Hochschule just before you started there. You must have heard something about him—he was the best violinist we had before he left Cologne, I say it freely. Not my style, perhaps, a bit on the superficial side for the classics, but he had tremendous facility, superb confidence and a real flair for the virtuoso repertoire. I heard him play an unbelievable Wieniawski F-sharp Minor Concerto at his graduation concert. Well, I always considered him one of my circle of friends—maybe not a close friend in whom I could confide, but a thoroughly pleasant fellow with whom I could always chat about music, our teachers, the profession. We never discussed politics, though, and now I'm glad about that.

What do you think I heard the other day? He's been cozying up to some big shots in the Party, playing dance tunes at their banquets in Berlin. The next thing you know, he'll show up at a Hitler Youth rally in the woods somewhere, playing the Chaconne for those little shits in front of a campfire. They'll all think they shared a deep spiritual experience, something that cemented the mystical "German" bond between them.

I can't understand what would lead Bremer to sell out. He should know better, and he's a good enough player that he doesn't need to do it for his career. I don't think he's anti-Semitic, not deep down, or he wouldn't have been friends with me; he must have known my background. I guess his ambition is a lot stronger than his conscience.

But here's an example of a different sort of fellow. Hugo Albers was one of the concertmasters in Berlin. I knew him before he got that job, from a chamber orchestra in Düsseldorf that I used to play in. We shared the first stand, and I always thought he was a bit of a stiff. Too serious, no spark of inspiration. You know the type— pencils always sharpened, bowings always worked out before the rehearsals. Whatever I thought of him as a colleague, though, I completely misjudged his qualities as a person.

I found out later that he was married to a Jewish woman, and they weren't getting along so well. Maybe that's why he was always so quiet, so reserved. Anyway, he was quite reliable as a concertmaster and even a decent soloist, absolutely solid technically. So I wasn't surprised when he got the job in Berlin—that's the kind of player they'd look for. Things were going well for him until the spring of last year, when the Ministry of Culture began to get very interested in the personnel of the top orchestras.

He was called to the manager's office, where a few officials from the ministry were waiting—I have this on good authority—and offered the chance to keep his position with a big pay increase if he would divorce his wife immediately. He told them he'd think it over. The next week he and his wife packed their bags and left for America. They got divorced within a month of their arrival.

I understand he's concertmaster in Baltimore now—a decent enough orchestra, I'm told. Nothing like Berlin, of course. But what should that matter to him? He can always move up over there, to New York or Boston, I suppose. And his hands are clean. That's the important thing.

I'm not sure you or I would have had the guts to do what Albers did. Believe me, I put myself in Bremer's place, and in Albers', and I don't know which of them I would have acted like if I'd been Gentile. These times bring out the best and worst in people. You find out the truth about them, and about yourself, too. For those of us caught somewhere in the middle, neither bastards nor heroes, maybe the best thing to do is to find a way out.

I have to be honest with you, Gottfried: when you tried to stop me from writing that letter to the Völkischer Beobachter, it made me think less of you. You were so worried I'd embarrass you in front of the strangers sitting across from us in the Goldener Adler. Maybe you thought there was a spy at one of those tables. Do you think it has come to that? Are there spies planted everywhere? Maybe by now that's true. Thank God I'm in England!

But what bothered me most was your insistence that since the Nazis don't have universal support, things will get better. How? How is that possible when they have Germany in a stranglehold? How will things get better without a war?

When we parted company that day, I was so glad I'd be leaving the country within a week. It's the passivity that I was so desperate to get away from, because I recognize the same thing in myself. I could no longer trust myself to be a decent human being if I stayed in Germany.

I think you're a talented violinist, Gottfried, and I look back fondly on some of the times we shared. But as

for the continuation of our friendship, I really don't know
what the future has to offer us.

Ernst

It was only after Gottfried tore up the letter and the envelope it came in that he wished he'd checked to see if anyone else had opened it first.

———————

Frankfurt. How different it seemed to him now. When he was there with the chamber orchestra a few months earlier, he had wandered dreamily in the Old City and walked for hours along the river, feeling as if the world was smiling at him that brisk, sunny day. His head and heart were full of Marietta, full of his new idea of playing recitals with her, fantasies of touring together: making music for hundreds of people and then making love in their hotel room.

Now he knew better, this cold, dreary afternoon in March. Four days ago she had given herself to him in his apartment in Cologne, but even if they were already married, they wouldn't be able to stay together in the same hotel anymore—her identity papers wouldn't pass muster in a respectable Aryan establishment. Now his eyes were open as he walked around. He saw banners with swastikas all over the place, and hastily skirted a street-corner rally where an SA officer was exhorting his countrymen to purify themselves and take charge of their destiny. He wondered why all the different people at such rallies were supposed to have only one destiny.

But the main difference in Frankfurt was not between a beautiful day and an ugly one, nor did it lie in his greater awareness of the Nazis. If the world seemed to have lost its innocence, it was because he had changed. He couldn't believe how naïve he'd been—he must have had blinders on.

Struggling against the wind, he went down to the river, hands thrust deep into his pockets, shoulders hunched up, his chin pulled down toward his chest. The water was churning with angry little whitecaps; the sky was opaque with dark clouds. He could have turned back toward his hotel, but kept walking farther and farther along the river even as freezing rain began to fall.

The difference was that a few short months ago, he had believed that if Marietta returned his love, he would be happy. More than that—he had believed the potential for immense happiness existed within him, had walked along this same stretch of river so convinced of his ability to love that nothing he could imagine would get in its way, unless his love were not returned. And that was why the world had seemed fundamentally good to him that day, despite its manifest evil, which even he wasn't blind enough to be totally unaware of.

Now he knew better. Marietta had returned his love, and had offered him a future that he wasn't prepared for—one whose requirements upset the comfortable fantasy he'd woven for himself. A few days ago she had hurriedly "married" him in his room in Cologne and then rushed off, sure of herself, purposeful, to catch the evening train back to Frankfurt—so her father wouldn't suspect what she had done. Things had to remain calm between them until after the audition.

Within the next few days, she assured him, she would get some forged documents to prove that he had a Jewish grandmother. Who would question them these days? After all, nobody would lie about such a thing unless it was in order to prove the *absence* of Jewish blood. The grandmother plus an imminent marriage to a Jewish woman (if somehow she could inform the jury members of their plans without her father's knowledge) should provide enough of a necessity to emigrate to Palestine: they would let him audition.

"No Aryan in his right mind would try to claim Jewish descent," she had said, laughing as she got up from his bed and began to button her blouse. There was a richness in the music of her voice that he hadn't noticed before, still bell-like but deeper: now it was the voice of a woman who had willingly and successfully passed from one stage of life to the next.

But he hadn't been able to make that passage with her. He wasn't sure if she had noticed, swept up as she was in her newfound power, the power of her sensuality so perfectly in tune with her emotions and even with her plans. At first his body had reacted eagerly enough to the warmth and softness of hers. He buried his face in the whiteness of her neck, inhaled the fragrance of her hair. His arms relaxed as they enfolded her; it was no longer an effort to keep his fingers from curling into a fist. Her beauty and his animal response to it were enough to distract him from the violent impulses that had clouded his mind a few minutes earlier. He was grateful to her for this, grateful there was no more talking, planning, nothing but the language of their bodies as they came together.

But then he began to think of Ilse, a violist in the chamber orchestra, who had been his girlfriend briefly the year before. She was completely different from Marietta—a big, buxom blonde, and they had shared the fleeting, purely physical passion of two acquaintances who decide to try it as lovers for a while. Her body had given him great pleasure, especially the rubbery resilience of her breasts. Sometimes he had her stand naked at the foot of the bed for minutes on end so he could gaze at her. He would imagine he was in some imperial garden, about to make love to a statue whose marble perfection had magically turned into flesh.

Suddenly he was afraid that if he didn't pretend Marietta was Ilse, he would lose his potency. This had happened to him occasionally with other women, though never with Ilse, and he was damned if he'd let Marietta see that side of him as well as all his other doubts. So he kept picturing Ilse as he moved on top of her. When it was over and they lay there spent, and her hands continued to explore his chest and belly, he felt cheated, as if this event he had so long dreamt of had passed him by and he'd barely experienced it.

It wasn't only Ilse that had distracted him. The memory of his meeting with Marietta's father had cast a shadow over their lovemaking. Only as her head rested on his chest and she fell asleep for a few minutes did Gottfried understand why he had gone to see him. Her father was right: it wasn't really in order to benefit the Jewish community, or even to get closer to Marietta through performing together. He had gone there in order to ward off a fear he couldn't fully explain to himself.

Something was happening to his playing. He'd never had so much trouble practicing, never felt so uninspired. Every day, as he took the instrument out of its case, he dreaded the fruitless repetitions, the sense that his work was going nowhere.

He had known that Herr Lupescu's approval was probably too much to hope for; he wasn't going to accept an Aryan into his family, not now. But Gottfried had wanted at least to avoid his disapproval. He would have welcomed some cue from him, no matter how indirect, that he was on the right path. Her father wouldn't be a member of the jury, but he might attend the auditions in an administrative role. Trying to sneak around him made Gottfried nervous, and he didn't need to be more nervous about this audition than he already was.

Of course, his attempt at bridge-building had failed and made things worse, wedging a guilty secret between him and Marietta. His visit had probably contributed to her father's complete rejection of their relationship. He felt a wave of resentment as he thought of him and the jury members, all Jews, sitting in judgment, perhaps in some corner of their minds holding him responsible for what was happening in his country.

Did the Jews secretly consider themselves superior to Aryans? he wondered. Germany had the tradition of great music, of course, but were the Jews more talented performers than "pure" Germans, better equipped to communicate that legacy to an audience, able to breathe life into it with more flair, more fluent virtuosity, more soul?

He thought of all the Eastern European violinists he had met, their Russian and Polish accents lending an air of worldly experience to everything they said about music. He remembered their easy, elegant way of spinning a phrase with that sumptuous "Russian tone." The violin seemed like a natural extension of their bodies; they had the ability not only to sing but also to speak through their instruments. He remembered the Jewish players from Hungary and Romania, the Gypsy influence, their "parlando-rubato" style. Even the native-born German Jews seemed to have imbibed some of that spontaneous approach with their mothers' milk.

They had centuries of suffering, displacement and adaptation in their blood. It was a potent brew. The German people's much-vaunted purity paled by comparison.

Ernst's story of the untalented pupil with the armband came back to him as he lay there with Marietta snuggled against him. He could almost see the boy's jaw jutting stolidly over the chinrest, the stiff motions of his arms, the back-and-forth straightening and bending of his right elbow failing to achieve any legato between the bow strokes. Gottfried could hear the squareness of his phrasing, the musicality "more appropriate for a marching band" than for a violinist.

Why was he thinking about that boy, he asked himself, why was he seeing and hearing him so vividly?

The wooden phrasing, the dry tone—was that what Ernst heard in his playing, too, even though he sometimes said that Gottfried was gifted?

Do they think we all sound like that?

He shifted abruptly in bed; Marietta stirred, stretched and began to whisper about their future together in Palestine. He found himself wishing she would just speak in a normal voice. No one was there to overhear them.

———————

Finally he turned back, drenched, shivering, and made his way toward the hotel. It was getting dark. His audition was at nine o'clock the next morning and he still had some practicing to do. He couldn't shake off the feeling that something bad was going to happen, but he wasn't sure what it would be. His Beethoven Concerto had been getting worse in the past week, not better.

Probably he would just get nervous at the audition and make a fool of himself, and that would be the end of it. Not the worst thing in the world, he told himself. It would be embarrassing, but it didn't really warrant the kind of dread he was feeling. It wasn't as if everything in his future depended on this one audition. Even without a job he could still emigrate to Palestine, find Marietta and marry her. As for his playing,

somehow he'd carve out opportunities; they could start playing together again, maybe in public this time, and if he was
lucky, music might feel the way it had before.

On the way back to his hotel he wandered into a church,
seeking a momentary respite from the wind and pouring rain.
It was quiet, dimly lit, if anything even colder than outside.
Fortunately there was no service in progress; he wasn't sure
why he had strayed in there, but he needed to be alone with his
doubts.

The soles of his shoes made a wet, splattering sound on the
stone floor. Moving slowly down the aisle, he heard the organ-
ist practicing. A Bach chorale filtered softly through the stillness, punctuated now and then by gusts of rain hitting the
stained-glass windows: "Jesu, Joy of Man's Desiring" wafting
across two centuries, beckoning to him from his childhood,
oblivious to the Nazi rally that had taken place that afternoon
just a few steps away.

"Music is my religion," he had told his parents when he
stopped coming to church with them at the age of eighteen.
They didn't understand; to them music was entertainment,
and whatever spiritual dimensions it was capable of could only
be revealed only in the service of faith. "What I experience
alone when I play the Chaconne by Bach means more to me
than sermons and ritual." They had shaken their heads in disapproval.

As he approached the altar, he realized that if music was
his faith, he no longer believed in himself as a musician. For
years he had thought that love and music would replace religion in his life. But if that were true, why was he going
through all this indecision, all this doubt about the path he'd
chosen with Marietta? Now he wondered if he had been over-
confident in his proclamation to his parents. When he stopped

coming to church, didn't that leave a void that he simply hadn't acknowledged until now?

Then he saw the life-size wooden figure on the Cross staring down at him. He took a step back. The sculpted Jesus, eyes half-closed in pain and resignation, filled him with a fear he couldn't understand.

Most people come here for solace, he thought, glancing at a hymnal lying open on a pew. He remembered playing the *St. Matthew Passion* a few months earlier with tears in his eyes, finally giving himself up to the story of the Crucifixion, with all its imagery and symbolism, permitting himself the luxury of faith only in the temple of great art. How uplifted he had felt!

He looked up again at the suffering face, which seemed to look back with reproach, but gently enough to hold out the possibility of forgiveness. It occurred to him that he might try to pray. He could see himself kneeling, asking for guidance at this turning point in his life, pleading for a strength he knew he didn't have on his own. But the problem was that he could see himself doing this as if he were watching another person. It would be like acting a scene from a play.

The music had stopped; the wind had abated somewhat. The rain had quieted down to a faint drizzle against the walls and windows of the church. In the silence he felt alone, more alone than he had ever felt, and suddenly it was too much to bear. He shuddered and walked quickly down the aisle toward the exit. Before leaving he turned around and looked at the crucifix once more, relieved that those eyes hadn't followed him.

Maybe I should think about coming to church again, he said to himself, and wondered what it would be like to attend church in Palestine, married to a Jewish woman.

———

The next morning he woke up early after a night of fitful sleep and a recurring dream in which he couldn't get to a concert on time. He found himself on the wrong train, got off and rushed across the platform to the right one, a number 3 in the dream, only to discover after a few stops that it was going in the wrong direction. After retracing his route, he finally got off at the right stop and hurried out of the station. As he was getting close to the hall where he had to play, he began to relax, his shoulders loosened up and he even felt a certain buoyancy, a carefree lightness in his limbs. Then he looked down at his hands and saw they were empty. He had left his violin on the train!

Totally unrefreshed, he pulled himself out of bed and managed a few unsteady steps across the room. There was a mirror just above the washstand. Usually he thought of himself as a rather handsome man, but he was shocked at the way he looked this morning. His eyes were smaller than usual, sunken, squinting, and there were dark circles beneath them. The wings of his nose looked bulbous and fleshy. His whole face seemed bloated, out of focus, as if he had a hangover. He turned away from the mirror in disgust.

He had no appetite, but forced himself to go to the breakfast room for some sustenance, to get some strength. His right hand shook as he poured himself a cup of coffee. If it was shaky now, he wondered, how would it be in two hours at the audition?

Why was he reacting this way? He sometimes got nervous, but never like this. Once again he tried to reason the fear away. He reminded himself that the audition shouldn't be a test of how well he played in general, but simply a step toward building a future with the woman he loved. Even if he didn't play his best—that was already a foregone conclusion—it could still go well enough for him to get a job in the violin section.

But such reasoning couldn't calm him down.

It was much too early to practice in the hotel. He had time to kill, so he decided to walk to the Jewish Academy, where the auditions were being held. Normally he would have taken a tram or a taxi. It was a long way and it was probably freezing outside, but at least that freezing rain had stopped, and he thought a vigorous walk might do him some good. He would still get to the academy early enough to warm up for half an hour.

Again he walked along the river, only in the opposite direction from the previous day. He had to navigate around huge puddles with patches of ice, and got aggravated when some mud spattered his shoes and the cuffs of his trousers. After getting splashed a couple of times he suddenly stopped caring, and instead of looking at the ground he looked straight ahead, westward along the river and at the buildings he was approaching.

I just want some peace, some freedom, he said to himself. He began to think of Palestine as he had pictured it in the Bible—which he hadn't read in years—and strained against his chilly surroundings to imagine palm trees and fragrant breezes. He thought of Jesus' betrayal and capture in the garden, and Pilate's equivocations and the Crucifixion. The words "Agnus Dei" ran through his mind along with some intricate, tortuous melodies from the alto aria in Bach's B Minor Mass, which he had recently played. He remembered several passages in the Old Testament about sacrificial lambs.

He thought about scapegoats, and the Jews of today, and then Marietta. It came as a shock to him that he'd hardly thought of her all morning. He was supposed to see her at his audition in less than an hour, the audition that would unite their lives. This was the woman he had slept with for the first

time a few days earlier, and had dreamt of sleeping with for
months, but somehow he couldn't picture her body now. He
could remember it only through words: he told himself that
she was slight of build, had firm skin as well as a womanly
softness, and her body seemed to store up great energy,
whether she was standing still, playing the piano or lying in his
bed. But when he tried to *see* her body—after all, it had been
early afternoon, and the sunlight was filtering through the cur-
tains of his bedroom window—he drew a blank, and when he
persisted in his effort, he began to see Ilse's statuesque body
instead. He wanted to banish Ilse from his mind but couldn't,
and when he tried at least to see Marietta's face, that too was a
great effort. He could remember the dark hair, the thick eyebrows, the full red lips, or rather could remember that she possessed those features, but couldn't put them together into a
recognizable face.

Frightened, he walked faster and was glad to see the building that housed the Jewish Academy not far away. But then—
later, he wouldn't have been able to describe what happened,
couldn't remember the exact sequence of his thoughts—he
began again to imagine a sacrificial lamb with a knife at its
throat and a basin to catch the blood. And a scapegoat cast out
into the wilderness to ward off the wrath of God. An innocent
creature on whose head a priest would pile the transgressions
of an entire people: the Jews may have devised that method to
cleanse themselves of sin, but it had been turned against them.
They had become an outcast nation, scattered across the globe,
blamed for everything real and imagined that had gone wrong
in the last two thousand years, from "ritual murder" and the
most recent economic depression all the way back to the death
of Christ.

He tried to picture Judas, tried to imagine what was going

through his head when he made that deal with the High Priests, and how he felt later, when he brought them to the garden with their soldiers and kissed Jesus so they would know whom to arrest. What drove him to do it? Was it jealousy—of the other disciples, or of Jesus Himself? An inability to accept Jesus' teachings, or a self-contempt so deep that he couldn't allow himself to belong to the community of the blessed and partake of salvation? Or was it simply that he had no choice in the matter, that he had been preordained for this hideous but necessary role in the history of the human spirit?

What would he have done in Judas' place? Gottfried asked himself. Would he have been able to resist such a powerful impulse to betray someone who loved him?

He thought again of the crucifix in the church the night before. He pictured it outside, up on a hill—as he'd seen the Crucifix in countless paintings—surrounded by a cluster of robed figures and Roman soldiers in breastplates and helmets. Only it wasn't Jesus hanging on the Cross, it was . . . a woman? He felt a twinge in his stomach when he realized it was Marietta he was imagining up there. Yes, he could finally see her naked body, but God, that wasn't how he'd wanted to see it when he was trying so hard to bring her into his mind's eye. He wrestled with that horrible crucifix, fought to push it away as he rushed along. Finally he succeeded: the figure nailed to the cross was no longer the woman he had claimed to love. There was no voluptuousness in that body—it was emaciated, bloody, faceless.

As he struggled with those images, he passed the academy without realizing it and walked on as if in a trance. The next time he looked at his watch it was nine o'clock, but he was outside the city limits. A church bell was ringing. He turned around and could barely make out the academy in the distance.

At first he thought of running back—maybe there was still time to rush in and try to explain. This had never happened to him before; he'd never been late to a rehearsal or an audition. Whenever he had dreamt of missing a concert or being unprepared, it had made him terribly anxious. But as the wind buffeted him on that river path, he felt oddly detached from any sense of urgency, and, for the first time in weeks, almost at peace with himself.

There was a small station near the river's edge, and he noticed a train approaching from the city. He made his way to the platform just as the train pulled in. Before he had time to think about it, he jumped aboard and sank into a seat with tremendous relief.

Only in the warmth of the carriage did he realize he'd been shivering. When the conductor came, he asked him how far the train would go, thinking it was just a suburban line. Cologne, the man replied; Gottfried laughed in surprise and bought a ticket. It occurred to him that he hadn't checked out of the hotel and some of his things were still there. That made him laugh again, until he noticed the few passengers scattered throughout the car looking at him. He pursed his lips and leaned his forehead against the window, watching the river and its fringe of bare-branched trees glide by as the train picked up speed.

Every day, he expected a telephone call, a letter, a reproach of some kind. But silence turned out to be more of a reproach than he could have imagined.

He thought she would try to reach him, maybe through a mutual friend, at least to make sure that nothing had happened to him. But she must have found out from his hotel that he had wired from Cologne that afternoon, settling his account and asking them to send on the things he'd left in his room.

For the first few weeks he couldn't practice, could barely bring himself to read a newspaper. The news was all bad, anyway. He had the feeling that events were rushing forward, and resourceful people adapted to them as best they could, while he hung back and did nothing.

There were so many times that he thought of picking up a telephone and calling her! So many times he almost did it, but held back at the last moment. What if her father were the one who answered the call? No, he didn't want to hear that mellifluous voice and those hard-edged words anymore. He began a dozen letters to her, but could find no way to explain what he had done. How could he explain it to her when he couldn't explain it to himself?

As the months passed, the only solace he could find, the only refuge from hating himself, was to imagine her safely en route to Palestine. He was relieved that she had left behind the hurt, the disappointment, the danger, and hoped she no longer reproached herself for the foolish choice she'd made to fall in love with a man like him. He could see her facing east, her lithe body leaning against the railing at the prow of the ship, her eyes scanning the horizon for some sign of a coastline, of a promised land that had not yet come into view.

Music was never the same for him after that. He did eventually find the courage to practice again; he hired an accompanist and played other pieces—he couldn't bear to rehearse any of the repertoire he'd worked on with Marietta. Those recitals and house concerts went passably well in the spring. But there was some fluidity lacking in his phrasing, some warmth gone, as if on that walk along the Main something had frozen in him forever.

XII

She glanced over her shoulder, then looked back at him shyly and came into the room. He closed the door, sat her down on his bed and offered her some of the coffee he'd been drinking. It must have been a luxury for her; she accepted it gratefully, and looked at him over the brim of the cup as she downed its contents. It was freezing outside, and she was shivering. He wrapped a blanket around her.

The hot liquid soon brought a hint of color to her cheeks. The skin was drawn tightly over the bones of her face, but there was something appealing about her. She must have been beautiful at one time. Her blue eyes were striking despite the shadows beneath them. Her lips, chapped and bitten, could have been voluptuous. Her hair—cropped short, of course—was reddish-brown. Auburn curls would have softened the angular severity of her features.

"What's your name?" he asked.

"Grete."

"Was it you who asked me to stay yesterday?"

She nodded, then spoke haltingly. "I wanted to apologize for this afternoon."

"It was my playing that led up to it. I should apologize to all of you for the way those guards . . . the way they rescued me. Were any of you badly hurt?"

She shook her head. "A lot of bruises, but nothing really serious. They must have been holding back."

If that was holding back, he thought—but said nothing.

"You must be wondering why I'm here." She looked down at the coffee cup cradled in her hands. "I . . . I had to talk to someone."

A few seconds went by; she seemed to need some encouragement. "I want to hear what you have to tell me," he said.

Grete put down the cup and faced the opposite wall as she spoke, sometimes half-turning to catch his eye. "Last night I couldn't sleep. The music you played kept running through my head. It reminded me of before . . . of life outside. And then I noticed there were no footsteps."

"Footsteps?"

"The guards pass near our barracks once every twenty minutes, like clockwork. I know because my bunk is closest to the door. At least two hours went by. I'd never dreamt I would miss that pacing, but when it wasn't there, all of a sudden the silence scared me. I thought it might be a trap, so I stayed in bed and finally fell asleep.

"Tonight there were still no guards around. I lay awake again for a couple of hours, but then I didn't see the point of waiting any longer, so I pulled the door open a few inches."

"Excuse me, Grete. I don't understand. They don't . . . lock you in at night?"

"The door is kept unlocked so we can use the latrine if we have to. The Kommandant made a point of that in one of his speeches to us about the special treatment we were getting. Besides, they're all obsessed with cleanliness. We're in a different area from the other Häftlinge, from where we used to be, and we don't have to work as hard. For the past few weeks they've been treating us . . . *well,* for some reason. Until this afternoon, which was an emergency. They're not going to change their approach tonight, I said to myself. What good would that do them? And if I'm wrong, what am I risking? If they shoot me, how many years of my life will I lose? How many *days?*"

She laughed bitterly and looked at him as if he would know the answer to that question.

"It doesn't make any sense to try to figure them out. I'm sure of only one thing: they never do anything by chance. Those guards were removed. So I'm probably doing what they want, but I don't care—as long as it doesn't endanger you."

"I don't think I'm in any danger," he said. Then he remembered that just before the war started, it was considered dangerous even to be seen with a Jew. After a while it was no longer an issue: the Jews had disappeared.

She studied his face for a few moments, as if to make sure she could absolutely trust him. "Sometimes a few of us talk about what we might do if we ever get out of here, but that's foolish. It can make you sick to think too much about the future when you know you'll probably never have one."

She bit her lower lip.

"Now and then we exchange a few words about what it takes to stay alive from one day to the next, but we can't talk about what it *feels* like to be here. They've taken away our language—I mean the language of the heart. And even if we could respond to things the way we used to, what would we say? There are no words to describe this. I can't explain it to you. You've been here only a few days, you haven't seen much yet, you couldn't possibly understand."

He wanted to say something, wanted to show her that he

could understand, or at least sympathize. But the haunted look in her eyes convinced him there was nothing he could say.

"We can't say how we feel. Maybe, if any of us survive— maybe later. But to tell someone even a small part of what's happened, to tell one's own story . . . You see, I don't know most of the other prisoners too well, not even the ones in the group that's getting special treatment. People you meet here you don't usually know for very long. And the people you knew before, like your family: either you don't know what's become of them, because you've been separated, or else . . . you do know."

She turned away from him; a vein was standing out on the side of her neck.

"I can't tell anyone here what I've seen. It would be a use- less repetition of their story, of what *they've* seen; it would be self-indulgent, a way of asking for sympathy. There's no place for sympathy here. Only an outsider, who understands maybe one-millionth of it, could feel an emotion like sympathy. And most of the outsiders who come here wear uniforms, they're the same as the guards, they feel nothing. But you're not like them—I know you're not."

He squeezed her hand.

"You know, before all this started, I wanted to become a writer." A hint of a smile flitted across her face. "It was just a young girl's fantasy, a dream of being famous someday. By the time I was fifteen, I'd filled three notebooks with poems and stories. They were realistic stories about everyday life, but they always seemed . . . so made-up to me. And now that whole pe- riod seems so remote, like a dream, like someone else's life. Now I've *lived* a story too horrible to be invented. Until today I never thought I'd find the words to describe what I've seen, or anyone to listen."

"Tell me now. Please."

It took her a few more seconds to summon the energy, or the courage, to begin. He knew it would be difficult for her to speak of these things, and for him to listen. But it was necessary for both of them.

"I come from Heidelberg. My father was a lawyer, and he taught at the university until 1933. He was able to continue with his law practice for about a year after he was dismissed from his teaching post. It took until the spring of '36 for my parents to realize that we absolutely had to get out of Germany. There could be no more waiting around and hoping for things to get better. But by then it was too late to get visas for all of us to enter the United States or England. We were put on waiting lists. After months of waiting we were turned down, and we couldn't even fill out applications for any of the other countries. They all had quotas for Jews.

"Then came that terrible night when they burned down the synagogues and smashed our shopwindows. Soon Germany's borders were closed to us. About six months after the war started, we went into hiding—my parents, my sister and I—in a Gentile friend's attic. For two years that man and his family risked their lives to feed us and keep us from going crazy with fear and boredom. You know, two years is a long time to be shut up in an attic, even with three people you love. It was hard to keep those walls from closing in on us. But every time we got on each other's nerves, we found a way to become cheerful and optimistic afterward. And we never had the courage to admit how forced that optimism felt.

"One day our friend and his wife and son disappeared. We didn't know if they left because they wanted to or if they were taken away for some political reason—surely not us, since we would have been taken at the same time. There was enough food left in our tiny kitchen to last a few days. Imagine the panic we felt at the idea of the food running out. But we were spared that agony, because the SS came for us on the third day.

"There was a door that had always been kept shut, except when our friends brought us food—the hidden door at the bottom of the stairway that led to our attic. I'll never forget the knocking on that door when they found us. We looked at each other without saying a word. I saw in my parents' and sister's eyes that they had always known this moment would come. All the hopes we had talked about, all the dreams of a peaceful life together after the war—all were false, a pack of beautiful lies we'd been telling each other. The pounding on that door was the truth tearing down the walls between us.

"I looked at my father's face as they started to kick through the door, as it cracked and began to give way. He hadn't acted soon enough to get us out of the country: I think the guilt he felt for that made him irritable most of the time. But when the door caved in and we heard those boots pounding their way up the stairs, his face looked strangely peaceful. It was over now, out of his hands. And as he looked at me, I felt such love for him.

"They dragged us downstairs and out to the street. Two vans were waiting. My sister was forced into one; the rest of us were shoved in the other. My sister, my poor, dear sister Nora: she had to face the beginning of the torture alone."

Grete swallowed audibly. "I've never seen or heard anything about Nora since that night. That was over two years ago. I . . . I doubt she's alive. But the idea of her sitting in that van alone, suddenly torn away from her family—poor little Nora, who was never so strong—that idea tortures me more than thinking she's dead. You know why? Because I can't imagine her alive anymore, can't picture her dealing with life in a place like this, with the hunger and fear and a hundred humiliations every day."

She paused, then suddenly turned to face him. "I'd rather have her be dead," she said fiercely. "She'd be better off. It would have to happen sooner or later, anyway. Why not sooner, when there's nothing to live for?"

Gottfried took her hand again, since he could think of nothing to say. After a few seconds she calmed down enough to continue her story.

"They took us to a detention camp not far away. The camp didn't have the proper 'facilities,' as they called them. Later I found out what that meant—no 'showers' or crematoria."

"Showers?"

"Yes." She withdrew her hand from his. "Didn't you know?" The nuance of irony in her voice made him uncomfortable. "That's their pet name for the gas chamber, their favorite method. You know the biggest building in this camp, the one with the chimneys?"

He wanted to get up and pull open the window.

"That's where they kill prisoners and dispose of the bodies after they've been gassed." Her tone of voice had become almost matter-of-fact. "Gas isn't used in warfare anymore. It's not fit for human beings; there are more dignified ways for them to die. But for us Jews it's all right. For the last two days, though, the furnaces have been shut down. No one knows why, but I'm sure of one thing. It's not out of the kindness of their hearts. There must be something wrong with the mechanism—maybe they're waiting for the engineers to come. Another thing I'm sure of: the chimneys may be quiet, but that doesn't mean the selections have stopped."

"Selections . . ."

"That's when they choose who's going to be killed."

How many . . . how many per day? The furnaces: overstuffed,
clogged—yes, that was a much more likely explanation for shut-
ting them than the Kommandant's "esteem for the arts."

"We had to wait at the transit camp until there was enough
room for us to be sent here. Meanwhile they made us work
twelve-hour shifts in a factory nearby. We ate something that
passed for soup and a piece of stale bread twice a day, and at
night we were all crowded into one large barracks with hundreds of bunks. Because the camp was much too small for all
of us, the SS didn't even bother to separate the men and
women. They kept saying we were there only temporarily. But
I knew that wherever our final destination was, things could
only get worse.

"I watched my father a lot during the days we spent in that
camp. He had that same peaceful look more and more, which
meant he wasn't responding to anything that was happening
around us. One day they shot a prisoner right in our room, for
some minor offense. I don't remember what it was, if it was
anything at all. Maybe the guards were just having fun. The
man fell a few feet away from my father, who sat on his bunk
with no reaction, at least none that I could see. Afterward he
never mentioned the shooting; it was as if it hadn't happened.
His eyes were far away and he hardly talked anymore. What he
did say didn't sound like him, didn't make much sense.

"And then I woke up one morning to my mother's screaming. She was shaking me, her nails were digging into my shoulders. I looked across at my father's bunk, but even before I
looked, *I knew.* I couldn't see his face because the blanket was
twisted, bunched up over his chest and head. One arm was
hanging from the bunk with a slash in the wrist. A razor lay on
the floor in a red puddle.

" 'No, it's a nightmare,' I said to myself. Then I saw some of the other prisoners looking at my mother and me. I pushed her hands away and jumped out of bed. I leaned over the top of the bunk, pulled off the soaked blanket and looked at my father's face—ashen skin, yellow lips, glassy eyes staring at the ceiling.

"I'm still not sure how he got ahold of that razor. He must have swiped it when his head was shaved soon after we arrived, when he still had enough presence of mind to be able to plan something. And somehow he'd managed to keep it hidden."

Grete reached for the coffee cup, which was on the little table next to Gottfried's bed, and took a few gulps; her mouth must have been terribly dry. Her hands shook as she put the cup down. She folded her arms and pressed them against her belly, her shoulders hunched over slightly, her head bowed. After a few moments she began again.

"I stood there stroking his cheek, struggling to breathe. My mother was still screaming, and there was a lot of noise as the others tried to make her stop. They didn't want trouble with the guards—they had to shout at her to get her to listen. Of course, the guards heard the commotion and came in. Suddenly everyone was quiet. I'll never forget that silence: it roared in my head like an ocean. Their leader looked at everyone standing near my father's bunk. In a few seconds he figured out what was going on. He turned to my mother and asked, 'Was this your husband?' His voice was *sympathetic*. She burst into tears again and nodded her head.

"My mother was a fool. She shouldn't have admitted anything. I suppose they could have looked it up in their records, but by then the bastard's whim might have passed. He clicked his tongue and said, 'It would be too cruel to let you outlive him in such grief.' Then he pulled out his gun and shot her."

Grete stared at the opposite wall of the room for a few moments.

"She was thrown backward onto the floor. I can still see the expression that was on her face for the few seconds before it went stiff. I tried to ignore the dark blotch that was spreading across her forehead, tried to look only at her eyes. She seemed . . . surprised. The guards laughed, and her murderer looked around and asked, 'Are there any other relatives of this man in the room?' I was so afraid that someone would give me away with a word or a glance. He stared at me for a long time. I was sure he knew, sure it was all over for me. I must have been white with fear, but somehow I kept quiet. Slowly, reluctantly, he put his gun away and left with the others. It was our job to drag my parents' bodies out for burial."

She swallowed with effort, her eyes squinting as she struggled to finish the story. Gottfried grabbed her hand. She sighed.

"I said my mother was a fool—she didn't know how to survive. My sister is probably dead, too. The only survivor in my family is me, why or how I don't know. I survived the horrible train ride, with hundreds of us crammed into freight cars for three days in the summer heat. The windows were boarded up. Once or twice, after hours without moving, we started up again in the opposite direction, as if they couldn't decide where to send us. All around me people collapsed from lack of water or starved to death. The smell . . . I can't describe it. Then the doors were pulled open the night we arrived here, floodlights in our eyes, guards shouting, dogs barking. I survived that first selection on the platform, too. And I've survived here until now. But maybe . . . maybe I'm the biggest fool of all."

Grete turned toward him, her eyes fierce blue beacons of pain. She was staring through him, through the wall behind him. Her jaw was quivering. When at last she was able to focus her eyes, she seemed to notice the look of horror that was frozen on his face, and broke down.

He put his arms around her, rocked her gently. Her tears soaked his collar. She released her grief in long, shuddering wails that were muffled by the pressure of her face against his chest. Between her sobs she gasped for breath.

He tried to say something to comfort her, but the movement of his lips produced no sound. Even if he had found his voice, what could he have said? He stroked her head, and suddenly ached to know what she had looked like before they did this to her.

Her hair—he wanted to run his fingers through the curls they had cut off.

Looking at the spare, gray-clad body pressed against him, he suddenly imagined the rosy tips of her breasts and a brush of coarse reddish hair between her legs.

Her father had killed himself, she had seen his bloody arm dangling from the bunk, and then her mother had been murdered in front of her. Her people were being gassed and incinerated. She had entrusted him with her story, he had listened in horror and sympathy, but now he couldn't banish the thought of her without clothes on.

How would that frail body react to a lover's caresses?

Then an idea passed through his mind—it seemed to come direct from the hellish world she had been describing. If he wanted to have her, he could. It didn't matter how she felt. If she didn't want him to take her clothes off or lie on top of her, *that wouldn't have to stop him.* She was too weak to resist. Who would know the difference? To whom could she complain? The Kommandant? Her fellow inmates, and admit that she had come to his room?

He looked down at the chapped, reddened hands that were resting in his. They felt bony, brittle. He eased his hands out from under them. The skin of her forearms was drawn tight; the elbows were sticking out. So were the bones of her face and the back of her neck.

The same odor of decay he'd noticed in the concert hall had permeated her clothes and skin. Her breath was fetid after so much talking and crying.

No, on second thought, she wasn't very desirable. Not in this condition. It even seemed strange that this creature was still alive, after all she had been through. And suddenly it *offended* him that she was still alive, that her skeletal frame had clung to life so desperately, that what was in front of him could still be called a human being. With feelings, with rights. He was seized by restlessness, especially in his hands—a need to move them, to grab something.

He was afraid of what his hands might do.

Her weeping had begun to subside. He got up, shoved his hands into his pockets and walked to the window. When he looked back, she was watching him.

"What's the matter?" she asked weakly.

He didn't answer for a few moments, struggling to keep his hands in his pockets.

"What's wrong?"

"I get dizzy sometimes," he said in a monotone, looking out the window. "There's no fresh air in here." He tried to open the window, but it was stuck.

"Maybe we should go outside."

He turned around, surprised.

She used the sleeve of her shroudlike garment to wipe away the last of her tears. "Sometimes you can walk a little, when you make sure there are no guards within a few hundred feet. All those nights when I couldn't sleep, I'd look out the window next to my bunk. I watched the guards patrol. I know where they walk, at least near our barracks; I know their rhythms. We'd have to listen for footsteps and stay within the shadows of the buildings."

He was still hesitating. "What one person can do alone may not be safe for two."

She looked at him for a few seconds, waiting to see whether he would change his mind. "Of course, I don't have much to lose. For you it's different, so maybe we should just . . ."

"No, no, you're right. Let's get out of here." He didn't want to be reminded of that difference between them.

He put on his overcoat and helped her bundle up in a couple of blankets before they left the room. As soon as they got outside, he was grateful. The cold air and biting wind were refreshing; the feeling of being boxed in began to give way. This was the first time since his arrival that the lingering smell from the chimneys seemed to have dissipated. Though it made him nervous to be walking with a prisoner, he tried to assume that his safety was guaranteed by the Kommandant—at least as long as he was useful to him. Maybe his presence could protect Grete as well.

He thanked God he was no longer caged in that room with her, struggling against impulses he could barely fathom. Whatever might happen to her in that camp, he knew she was no longer in any danger from him. For a moment he saw the two of them as if from a distance: a man and a woman clinging to each other as they groped their way through the darkness. They were figures in a nightmare landscape, each trapped in a different way.

The minute after this vision passed, though, it seemed like

an excuse he had concocted. Sure, blame everything on the camp. Under normal circumstances he was pure, decent.

What about that walk along the river in Frankfurt?

Suddenly she tugged at his sleeve and pointed to the main gate, which was still a fair distance from them. It was open— that was clear enough in the moonlight—and there didn't seem to be any guards around. The big searchlights had been turned off; the darkened watchtower looked empty. The camp was deathly still.

The moonlight, filtered through a passing cloud, lent a silvery shimmer to the iron archway. Beyond the open gate, glistening snow-covered fields and a pine forest beckoned.

I'll instruct the guards to open the gate for you immediately. A bluff. And then he had protected his precious experiment with threats about the Gestapo. But in the meantime Gottfried had played two more concerts, had pulled the prisoners more than halfway "back to life from this living death." The Kommandant could afford to let go of him now. He must be testing him to see how serious he was about leaving.

The Kommandant knew that Grete was with him; Gottfried was certain of that. She was right—nothing here happened by chance, or out of the goodness of their hearts. Everything was part of the experiment: They were rats in the maze he had designed. He had let her come to Gottfried's room, believing she was acting on her own impulse, and now he wanted to see if she was "truly alive" enough to venture through that gate.

Gottfried tried to explain all this to her. She looked at him doubtfully.

"We just have to walk through," he whispered.

"Those will be the last steps we ever take if it's a trap," she said, clutching his shoulder. "I know their ways better than you."

"But that's the risk we have to run, don't you see? And it might be more of a trap for you if we stay inside. He believes in the survival of the fittest, in Darwin's theory of evolution applied here and now to human beings. Only those willing to walk through the gate to freedom, with all its risks, deserve to be free—that's the way his mind works. Walking through might be your only chance to get out alive."

"You haven't lived this nightmare long enough. God knows what's really going on here. But even if you're right, I can't walk out alone. The others have to be told."

He couldn't believe she would even consider that. "Two might slip through, if it serves a purpose for the Kommandant. But thirty? He'd never take that kind of risk."

"Remember, we have nothing to lose. Anyone who might accept your explanation of this open gate is entitled to know about it. Most of them wouldn't attempt it, anyway. I'm sure of that. If you're worried about being part of a group, you can go through by yourself."

He was holding her thin arms just above the elbows, unwilling to relax his grip. He didn't want to be left alone, didn't want to decide on his own whether or not to take that chance.

"You can hide in those woods across the road until I find you. There's a small clearing about two hundred feet west of the gate—I used to pass it every day when they marched us to the factory. If I don't come within half an hour, forget about me and leave."

"Why do you have to go back to them?" The bitterness in his voice surprised him. "You said you never even talk to each other about anything important. What do you owe those people?"

She glared at him. He had taken her too literally, had dared to question a bond between them that he couldn't begin to understand. He let go of her; his arms dropped to his sides.

She turned and walked away briskly. For a moment he stayed there, angry at her, and thought of going through the gate by himself and *not* waiting for her in the woods across the road. It probably wouldn't be safe to wait.

But it was impossible to leave without his violin, anyway. How could he have forgotten the instrument that those wealthy patrons—some of them Jews—had helped him purchase back in 1935? You don't leave behind a priceless Guarnerius. Not when there's a choice. He hurried back to his room to get it.

Within five minutes he was making his way toward the gate again, violin in hand, but slowed down when he realized that without Grete he had no reason to take such a risk. Where could he go if he walked through that gate without express permission from the Kommandant? Surely not home. If he stayed just one more day and played the final concert, they'd drive him home and life would continue as before. Unless . . .

You have seen this place.

He turned a corner, only to see the beam of the searchlight sweeping across his path. Before the light could trap him in its pitiless glare, he hid behind the same warehouse he'd found the previous day, with its obscene cache of shoes. He tried to catch his breath.

Peering around the side of the warehouse, he saw that all the guards were in place. The gate was closed again.

What kind of goddamn trick are they playing on us? He waited until the searchlight was pointed away from him, then turned and hurried toward the prisoners' barracks to warn them. If thirty of them appeared at the main gate now, there would be a massacre.

The gate to the inner area of the camp was still unguarded. After a few moments' hesitation, he pushed it open. The ground was uneven, muddy. He lost his balance several times as he walked, trying not to run, hoping not to be too obvious a target if there were any guards around. It was all he could do to keep from falling, especially when he stepped deep into a frigid puddle. His shoes and socks were suddenly drenched. Stunned by the cold, he almost dropped his violin. He slowed down, staggering along, cursing under his breath, and finally stopped.

He thought he heard guards marching toward him, but it was only the blood pounding in his ears.

Then he heard a murmur of hushed voices. Looking through the window of a nearby hut, the only structure in the area that was lit from within, he recognized some faces from his group. Approaching the door, he heard the other prisoners arguing with Grete about the open gate—whether or not it was a trap and he was some sort of bait. When he entered the room, it was suddenly silent.

"It's too late," he said, struggling to catch his breath. "The gate's closed again. The guards are back in place."

"Well, he's here, telling us about it," said Grete to the others. "That proves he's not trying to lead us into a trap."

Some of the men closest to the doorway were looking at him, their eyes narrowed to slits of mistrust. He wished he could reach out to them, but it seemed too difficult. Maybe later . . . if there would ever be a "later." His eyes found the full-breasted woman standing among some of the others in the middle of the room. In the dim light of a single candle flickering near her on the floor, her ghostlike pallor reminded him of the corpses in his dream.

He glanced back at the men near him, tried to *see* their faces, but they looked like gray masks. Impenetrable, not quite human. Not in the same way he had thought when he first saw them. That was shock, and he was almost used to looking at them by now. Hollow cheeks and dark circles beneath sunken eyes could no longer shock him, but what he noticed now for the first time was how their noses protruded, beaklike, from a background in which all the other features seemed to have collapsed inward. They looked like birds of prey, like vultures.

But they are the prey, he tried to remind himself. *The corpses on which the real vultures, the ones in uniform, feast.* There were ugly bruises on some of their faces from that afternoon's assault by the guards. If he was searching for any common ground with them after what Grete had told him, any shared impressions of life, whatever each of them had experienced in the camp seemed to block the way.

He didn't want to speak to those people any longer, though he could well understand their mistrust. He took half a step toward Grete, but she backed away. Was she still angry with him for what he'd said near the gate? No, he decided, she just couldn't come with him now, while the others were watching. Besides, what connection was there between them? She had just wanted to talk, nothing more.

He returned to his room, lay down, waited for sleep. Dozing off from time to time, he would wake up with a start at some imagined sound. A guard passed near his window several times. He was freezing; his feet had been wet for fifteen minutes before he'd had a chance to dry them. And he had no blankets now—Grete couldn't very well have returned them to him in front of the other prisoners. His coat made a poor substitute for a blanket.

As the hours passed, he tried to concentrate on the Bach partita he was planning to play the next day, tried to hear it in his head, or at least to remember the fingerings and bowings he would use. But it was difficult to maintain his focus on the music, or on any subject, any logical chain of thought: Grete's story kept coming back to him, a host of horrific images whirling through his brain.

He fell asleep for an hour or two, but woke up long before dawn, his mouth terribly dry. Moving his tongue around in an attempt to moisten his lips, he groped for the glass of water he had left on the small table next to his bed. Suddenly he could see Marietta, could picture her more clearly than he had in years—the dark, curly hair pulled away from her face, the full lips, the look of energy and determination as she spoke to him. And he remembered how he had walked out of her life in that cowardly trance.

Ten years ago, as he trudged along that icy, muddy river road in Frankfurt, the landscape of his life changed forever. It seemed now as if very little of real importance had happened to him since then. Of course, the war had started a few years later, everything had changed around him, the world was falling apart. But in his life, there was a frozen walk along the Main, then like a sleepwalker he'd boarded that train and it had brought him . . . *here.*

He got out of bed and looked through his window at the internal fence and the ugly, squat buildings beyond, lit with relentless clarity by the glare of the searchlight each time it swept past his room. He leaned his forehead against the window, staring at the ground with its patches of snow, ice and mud until the glass frosted over with condensation from his breath.

XIII

"May I ask, sir, what's going to happen to them once I leave?"

"Why is that important to you?" He lit a cigarette, studying Keller's face as he inhaled.

"At first . . . they seemed like a bunch of corpses to me." As he searched for words, the Kommandant's face disappeared behind a small cloud of smoke. "They had no response to my playing, and I just wanted to get away. But they've changed so much. And I've changed."

The smoke thinned out, and the steel-gray eyes were still there, boring into him.

"How do I face them today, knowing I'll never see them again? Knowing they may never hear another note of music?"

The first day, the Kommandant had gone on and on; today he wasn't saying anything. It didn't feel right, talking to a stone wall, but somehow Keller had to spit out what he'd come to say. He glanced at the door, then turned back to face him.

"The war can't go on much longer, Herr Kommandant." His mouth had gone dry, and it was hard to articulate the words.

The Kommandant's eyes seemed distant now, veiled behind the thick lenses of his glasses. He was staring at a memorandum on his desk. Keller could make out the letterhead: the SS Main Office of Economics and Administration, Section D.

The inspectors from Oranienburg don't get here too often, so I can be flexible and pursue my scientific interests. But what decree from Oranienburg was weighing on him now? The corners of his mouth were tugging downward; his face seemed more lined than it had the other day. For the first time, Keller noticed dark pouches beneath his eyes.

He cleared his throat. "Later, it might help you to claim you saved thirty Jews."

The Kommandant looked up at him. "What did you say?" His eyes had regained their focus.

"If you're ever held responsible for what happened here . . ."

"What makes you think you have a right to talk about such things to me?"

"I'm sorry, sir, but I've been driven past too many bombed-out factories. I've seen whole towns leveled." The words were coming faster now, accelerating into a breathless cascade. "Schools, churches, everything turned to rubble. And the front is getting closer."

"Do you know what would happen if you implied in any public place that Germany might lose the war?" But his voice sounded tired, and the severity in his tone seemed forced.

Keller was determined to go on, to push through his fear. "This isn't a public place. I'm trying to speak to you . . . as one realist to another. If thirty is too large a group, I beg you to save a few, or just one. If it has to be only one . . ."

"I refuse to discuss any ideas predicated on the defeat of the Fatherland."

"What about the experiment? You've gone to so much

trouble to make it work. Don't you want to see if they can ever behave like normal people again?"

The Kommandant's laugh was dry, raucous. "Tell me, what is normal behavior these days?" He got up, walked over to the window and looked out. After a few moments, without turning back to face Keller, he said in quiet, measured tones, "I can only assure you that I'll do everything in my power to fulfill your wishes."

He kept staring out the window in the direction of the stone building with the chimneys, puffing away at his cigarette, enveloping himself in a blue-gray cloud of silence.

For the rest of the morning Keller thought about the Kommandant's cryptic promise to fulfill his wishes. It had come so abruptly, with his back turned, through a veil of smoke. There was nothing specific in his pledge, little for Keller to hold on to as he prepared for the final performance.

Yesterday he had saved the Jews from a massacre. So perhaps it wasn't such a huge leap to imagine he would continue protecting them, whatever his reasons. Of course, this was the man who had lied to him so smoothly about the inmates' shoes—and the ovens. But maybe he *had* to lie that first day.

The Kommandant had needed him to perform as well as possible in the experiment. If Keller had known the full truth from the beginning, his cooperation would have been half-hearted at best. And that wasn't good enough. The Kommandant had made it clear: he didn't want him just following orders.

Keller despised himself for trying to justify the man's lies, but he had to find a way to trust him now. He had to believe they had a chance. To bring them back to pain and terror was to bring them only halfway. The Kommandant must know that. If that was all he wanted, then this experiment was hardly worthy of the name—it would have to be considered a mere variation on the theme of cruelty, a refinement of torture. No, he must be looking for more than a sudden release of inhibitions, a momentary catharsis. The key to the whole experiment was *today's* concert, after the dam had burst: would they go wild again, would they slide back into lethargy, or would they listen with deep concentration?

Keller chose to believe the healing process had continued overnight.

It would take time to analyze the results of the experiment, to make detailed observations of the Jews' behavior in the coming days. Time was the precious commodity he had to purchase for them with his playing. Time was running out for the Third Reich.

———

That afternoon he played only one piece: Bach's monumental Partita in D Minor. The crowning glory of this work is the Chaconne, the culminating movement, longer and weightier than the first four movements combined. Thirty-two variations are built on a simple bass line. There are radical changes of mood—sweeping climaxes are followed immediately by the softest imaginable utterances—but the continuity is never broken. The music moves from urgency to repose and back again, never straying from its key, reworking the same harmonies in ever-shifting guises. It is full of the joys and sorrows of this life, and a yearning for something beyond.

Though a few of the prisoners stared at him when he arrived, most of them behaved like a normal concert audience. Speaking quietly among themselves, they settled down quickly to hear him play. Whatever their feelings were toward him, they seemed to need the music he was about to give them. He was sure there would be no screaming or violence.

Before he started, his eyes found Grete's. From the openness of her expression, from the expectant half-smile playing around the corners of her lips, he could tell she was no longer angry about the disagreement they'd had near the open gate. Before that, he had given her the sympathy she needed. He hadn't taken advantage of her weakness. Thank God, she had no way of knowing what had gone through his mind in that room.

The prisoners were not the only ones who seemed different. As he began the Bach, he was happy to hear how much his playing had changed. The sound was pouring out of his instrument. The violin seemed like part of his body; he held and moved around it without effort. The ebb and flow of the music rocked, soothed, almost hypnotized him. The phrasing was so natural—nearly speechlike—that he couldn't believe it was coming from him. All those measures he had practiced endlessly for purity of sound and intonation suddenly seemed *improvised,* as though the music were unfolding at that instant for the very first time. Yet the structure of the work had never been clearer to him.

At first he kept asking himself why it was happening. At last, what he'd always longed for. It all fit together—it was perfect, but how could it be? Without understanding what might have produced such a change, how could he hold on to it? It would slip through his fingers; the next performance wouldn't be like this.

Then he saw that there could be no assurances. For some reason a moment of bliss had been granted him, and it was worth any disappointment he might feel later. He wanted to savor every fraction of that precious moment, didn't want it ever to end. But within a few minutes he learned to stop worrying, stop thinking, stop trying to feel a certain way. It might be over in half an hour, yet there was so much in that piece, so many events that seemed sufficient to fill a lifetime, as long as he could invest them with enough meaning. So much *did* happen in that performance, and it was all recorded perfectly in his musical memory. For once, he had no doubts about the accuracy of his perceptions; he would always remember every phrase, every nuance.

When he finished, there was silence—a silence of awe, as though they were all possessed by the echo of that immortal music resounding through their souls. He stood there shaking, still in the grip of that final, inevitable cadence on D, a unison that seemed to stretch infinitely beyond its duration. Then came a burst of applause. It was thunderous, despite their small numbers and the dead acoustics of that place. He bowed low, knowing that once this applause stopped he would pack up and leave, and never see these people again. They had shared something unforgettable, and he couldn't bear the thought of returning to the drudgery of life as it was before.

While his head was still down, the door swung open. At least ten guards rushed in. The applause stopped. They grabbed a man sitting in back and pulled him over to a wall.

Three of the guards began to beat the man with their clubs. At first they weren't hitting him with all their strength. They were just fooling around: their ruddy faces took on a heightened glow, their smiles and laughter bespoke a game. In fact, it was the first time Keller had seen any of them smile. Nothing to worry about yet, he tried to tell himself. But then with a twinge in his gut he remembered seeing his family's cat play with birds or mice it had caught, administering what were little more than love pats to its terrified prey, sometimes even letting the injured victim move away a few inches before pouncing on it and breaking its neck with a powerful swat.

They were starting to hit harder now. The man screamed for help, tried to defend himself. His right arm got in the way of their clubs, then hung loose as the blows centered more and more on his head and neck. Red rivulets flowed from his nostrils into his mouth, where a rust-colored froth bubbled and gurgled as he struggled for air. He must have been blinded by the blood streaming down his forehead into his eyes.

Why him? Keller thought, unable to move. He was pretty sure the poor man was the one they'd dragged in the other day, the one who had hidden under his bed. But could that boycott of his concert have led to this?

Begging for mercy, the victim reeled and staggered from one to another of his torturers, as if he were approaching each of them in a hellish merry-go-round and waiting to be hit so he could move on to the next. They waited a little longer now between each time they struck him, giving more focus and emphasis to their blows. Their laughter had stopped, the smiles had faded from their faces. It was work now. Finally one of them, who seemed a bit more authoritative than the others, dropped his club. On his face was a look of boredom, even irritation with this tiresome Jew for putting them through such a tedious exercise. The Jew was taking too long to die.

The guard took out his pistol, pushed the tottering victim to his knees and put the muzzle to the nape of his neck. The poor man might have been praying for the last second of his life; his blood-flecked lips were moving rapidly, soundlessly when the shot came. As he pitched onto the floor, another guard gave him a final kick so vicious that the body rolled over and landed on its back.

Half the face had been blown away. Blood and brain tissue spattered the floor and the boots of his murderers.

The guards turned to the other inmates. In their stony faces, in those icy eyes was a death sentence with no possibility of appeal. And from the victims, mute fear. Keller would have expected screams, but all he heard was the blood pulsing in his head.

The guards lined up the prisoners and marched them outside. He rushed after them. It had just started to snow, and the wind was whistling in the distance. The prisoners were quickly arranged in rows of seven or eight. Some of the women were moaning now, others shivering audibly from cold and fear. Most of the men stared with sullen hatred at the guards. A few were praying, rocking from their heels to the balls of their feet as their heads bobbed.

The guards chose five men and three women and placed them against the wall of a neighboring building. The full-breasted woman was among them, her hands clasped, her face gaunter than ever.

A hunchback hobbled up to face the line of prisoners. Rudi had never finished telling Keller about him, but now he saw that the man was carrying a submachine gun, not a broom. Even though he wore the same kind of uniform as the guards, Keller couldn't believe he was one of them. He had never seen him together with the others, and would have thought him too deformed to qualify as a soldier of the Third Reich.

The man was hideously ugly. His nose must have been broken many times—probably from brawling in barrooms and back streets, Keller thought—and dense stubble darkened his face.

A few of the people against the wall were whimpering and

wringing their hands. One man was on his knees, begging for mercy. A guard grabbed his shoulder and jerked him back to a standing position. The hunchback pulled his right foot back, getting ready to shoot, but before he raised his gun Keller moved forward a few paces—not directly between him and his victims, but close enough to distract him. For several seconds the hunchback looked alternately at Keller and at the Jews lined up against the wall, blinking his dull eyes as he ran his fingers gently over the barrel of his weapon. A drop of spittle glistened on his lower lip.

"*Geiger!*" An Oberscharführer started to walk slowly toward Keller, his right hand resting on his holster.

Keller's heartbeat pounded like a drum in his head. "Are you sure . . ." he began, but his voice came out as a whisper.

"Yes?" The bully stopped, cocking his head. "Come on, speak up, I couldn't hear you." He started to pull his gun out.

There was no turning back now. Keller forced the words out because he had no other choice. "Are you sure the Kommandant would approve of this?"

The man's eyes widened, his features froze. Keller was sure he was about to be killed, could almost feel the bullet ripping through his head. But the Oberscharführer's hand seemed to hesitate, his gun suspended halfway out of its holster, as if he was calculating how far he could act on his own, just how far the violinist's immunity extended. Then his jowls began to quiver, his eyes lit up and he broke out in a loud laugh. His hand dropped to his side and the gun slid back into its holster.

As the other guards joined him in his ugly laughter, Keller began to breathe again. Maybe he would get out alive. But he couldn't forget why he was standing there. He swallowed, tried to steady his voice.

"I mean, he has gone to great lengths to make this experiment work, to see if he could change . . ."

"You have obviously misunderstood the experiment, Herr Geiger."

The smile disappeared from his face. He looked for a moment at the other guards, who quickly stopped laughing. Then he turned to the hunchback. "Come on, Karlchen. Ignore him, he's a fool."

Karlchen just stood there, squinting, visibly thrown off balance by Keller's intrusion. Maybe there was still a way to stop this. But Keller was sure that if he said any more, it would push the Oberscharführer's patience to the limit.

"Get out of the way," the big man said quietly, and there was more menace in those softly spoken words than there had been in his swagger and sarcasm.

Keller stood there a moment longer, knowing that the time to act was passing, had probably already passed. A guard had begun to move slowly toward him.

Suddenly there was a sound of running footsteps. He turned halfway around. One of the Jews was trying to get away.

The hunchback was faster than the guards; he fired without even pausing to take aim. The man fell, writhing and clawing the ground for a few seconds. Then he was still. The executioner lowered his gun and leaned on the butt with satisfaction.

"And now," he said to Keller, echoing the Oberscharführer, "will you get out of my way?"

The guard who had been inching toward them suddenly jumped and knocked Keller to the ground. The violinist struggled to free himself from the man's weight, tried to roll over and get up, but the guard was too strong for him.

He heard a burst of noise like the sputtering of a car engine that won't turn over, only much louder. It lasted little more than a second.

Seven corpses lay against the wall.

The hunchback lowered his gun with a flourish, and the guards congratulated him on his performance with genuine enthusiasm. Then he limped away, leaving the rest of Keller's audience huddled in the space between that wall and the next barracks.

The guard who had jumped on Keller pushed him out from under him and stood up, muttering "Jew-lover."

Staggering to his feet, Keller tried for a moment to hope that the other twenty would be spared. Or at least Grete, if he could get to the Kommandant before it was too late. But in his heart he knew that the killing was not yet over just because the crooked man had left.

"Now it's time for a visit to the cemetery," said the Oberscharführer, tapping his thigh with his truncheon. "We have to pay our respects."

The remaining prisoners were forced to drag the bodies down the long row of barracks, away from the "concert hall" and the main gate. The guards walked alongside them, beating them when they slackened their pace, laughing at their cries. Keller followed hesitantly, not knowing what to do, then quickened his pace and tried to get near Grete.

She was looking straight ahead as she marched. Tears streaked her face. She took no notice of him, didn't seem to hear when he called her name. The guards wouldn't let him get close enough to her.

He stood still for a few seconds while the others trudged forward. He wished he could grab her, pull her away. He had to speak to her, at least, couldn't just let her disappear from his life without another word exchanged.

As he rushed toward them, a guard saw him coming and shoved his gun butt into Keller's ribs. He dropped to his knees, gasping. Another guard ran over and kicked him in the groin. Waves of pain shot through him as he fell backward. Writhing on the ground, he saw the gleam of triumph in the man's eyes.

Suddenly Rudi's face hovered above him. "You fool," he whispered. "Are you trying to get yourself killed?" He grabbed Keller's shoulders with surprising strength to stop his thrashing around. "Don't try to save them. Nobody can."

But the pain in his belly made Keller too angry to care what might happen. He wriggled free of Rudi's grip, pushed himself up off the ground and went limping after them.

He caught up by the time they reached the burial ground. Approaching the edge of the yawning pit, he stopped and groped in his pocket for a handkerchief to cover his nose and mouth. Then he took a few steps forward.

If it hadn't been for the stench, he wouldn't have believed his eyes. Thickets of limbs protruded from piles of shriveled corpses. Eyes open, staring. Mouths agape, twisted, frozen in a chorus of silent screams.

No, this can't be real, it must be a nightmare.

But that was what Grete had said when she saw her father's body.

Please, God, let it be a nightmare, this whole thing, let me wake up and have it all be gone, even if . . . even if Grete doesn't exist.

The Jews threw the bodies in after stripping them. Then the guards ordered one of the prisoners to take off his clothes and jump into the pit. At first Keller didn't understand what they wanted of the man, but then it became hideously clear: he was expected to have sex with a female corpse.

They were pointing at the one with large breasts, bloody

from the wound in her throat. The other Jews drew back from the edge of the hole, but the guards forced them to watch. The man looked up at the guards, the purest hatred on his face as he spread her legs apart.

Is he going to give them what they want? Why even go through the motions when he must know they'll kill him anyway?

"Come on, Jew," said the Oberscharführer. "We haven't got all day."

But the man in the pit shook his head slowly and refused to get on top of the corpse after all. Once again the Oberscharführer pulled his gun halfway out of its holster, then seemed to decide on a change of tactics.

"Your life will be spared." But the lying promise was too blatant. The Jew continued to shake his head.

"What's the matter, Judenschwein?" sneered a guard from the other side of the pit. "Are you a faggot?"

The Jew turned calmly to face him and spat at his boots.

Keller spun around and ran toward the Kommandant's office, stumbling past barracks, avoiding clusters of guards who turned and looked but didn't try to stop him. The pain in his ribs and belly and the throbbing in his head slowed him down; he had to stop near the concert hall to gulp some freezing air.

When he reached the office, the guard posted there wouldn't let him in. Keller hesitated, wondering if he should attempt to argue with him. Instead he hurried around the corner of the building and came to a window through which he could see the Kommandant writing at his desk. He rapped at the window, but the Kommandant didn't look up. Keller rapped louder and louder until his fist smashed through the glass.

Now the Kommandant looked at him, with the same bored expectation Keller had noticed on his face the other day.

"How can you let them do this?" Keller said, his voice too soft, devoid of emphasis as he struggled to catch his breath.

Smiling, the Kommandant leaned back in his chair, crossed his legs and laughed. Yes, laughed: he found it amusing. His thin frame began to shake, and he pulled a silk handkerchief out of his pocket to dab his eyes. After a few seconds he leaned over the desk and started writing again.

Keller couldn't keep himself from smashing another windowpane. Blood spurted onto the sill. The Kommandant looked up again, sharply this time, his lips drawn into a razor-thin line. In his flinty eyes there was no trace of the hilarity that had convulsed him a moment earlier. Keller backed away. The Kommandant stared at him until he turned around and ran back toward the other end of the camp.

The guards and prisoners were returning. They stopped in front of the building with the chimneys and the condemned were ordered to strip. Some of them refused, but the guards tore off their clothes.

Twenty skeletal bodies shivered in the biting wind. The guards poked their gun butts into ribs and genitals, and pinched the women's buttocks. Then they stepped back. They're going to shoot them now, Keller thought. But nothing happened. Within a few seconds he understood the game they were playing: their victims would have to stand there for a while, freezing.

The minutes passed. The snowfall was thickening; everything was silent except the howling of the wind. Those poor emaciated bodies were turning blue.

"Grete!" he yelled, almost choking on the name.

A guard turned to him and barked, "Shut up!"

The girl looked at him as if from far away, from the other end of the universe. There was no fear in her eyes, yet her gaze wasn't dull. She seemed to understand what was happening, but she was beyond all of it. The tears on her cheeks had dried.

Some of the others were covering their genitals with their hands. Their moaning combined with the whining wind in a bleak dialogue Keller would never forget. But Grete was silent, and her hands remained at her sides.

Suddenly a prisoner pointed a finger at him and shouted, "It's your fault!"

A gust of wind slapped him in the face. "What? Why?"

"Your beautiful music was a dirty trick."

"But I didn't know it would come to this. Oh, God. Grete, tell them I didn't know!"

She looked at him again and said nothing. Wherever she was, wherever her spirit was traveling, it didn't matter whether or not he was guilty. He tried to look only at her face, but from time to time his eyes dropped. Her breasts hung like deflated balloons over the craggy protuberance of her rib cage. His gaze followed the contour of her swollen belly toward the darkness of the groin. It seemed wrong to look at her like that. But he wasn't watching her as the guards were, with an intent to humiliate; he was just trying to remember what it had been like to hold that frail body in his arms.

It was beginning to get dark. The sound of chattering teeth against the cries of the wind grew unbearable. How long were those pigs going to torture them?

And what will happen to me now that I've witnessed this?

Keller gagged as he swallowed a chunk of congealed saliva. He turned away and opened his mouth wide, trying to focus his eyes on the elaborate patterns made by the swirling snowflakes. Suddenly he heard a choked cry, then a high-pitched gasping for air. A man in the line of victims was swaying, tottering, one hand clutching at his throat. After a few seconds his knees buckled and he fell forward.

"Get up!" snapped a guard. The man didn't move. The guard and a couple of his cronies turned to Rudi, who was also facing the prisoners but was standing slightly apart from the line of torturers, hands thrust deep into his pockets, eyes trained on the ground as if he were fascinated by the whiteness of the snow accumulating there. He had been on the fringes of the grim procession to and from the burial pit, but so far he hadn't done anything.

He stiffened when he sensed that they were looking at him. Without words they seemed to be saying, "It's your turn now." Rudi walked over to the man on the ground, slowly pulled out his service revolver and fired a bullet into the man's head. The body jerked once from the impact, and the snow around the head began to turn crimson.

As he rejoined the line of guards, his eyes met Gottfried's for a moment, but he quickly looked away.

Five minutes later a man standing next to the corpse yelled, "Enough, you animals! What are you waiting for?" Some of the guards laughed quietly. Muttering curses, the man started to walk slowly toward the fence.

They let him walk at least half a minute. Finally he began to run.

Keller wanted so much for him to make it, even though he knew the man would be skewered on the barbed wire. In those last few seconds it was somehow obvious from the *way* he ran, the way his matchstick arms pumped the air as his spindly legs carried him forward, that he had begun to hope. He must have known better, of course, but at that last moment a mindless survival mechanism seemed to propel him.

They shot him just as he reached the fence.

After ten more minutes, some of the prisoners were begging to be killed. Finally the Oberscharführer announced, "All right. It's time for your hot showers now," and opened the door of the building. The Jews rushed inside. Several guards went in with them. The door was closed.

The other guards went their separate ways, leaving Keller alone outside the death factory. He stepped back a few feet and threw himself at the entrance, but he knew there was nothing more that could be done for her. Exhausted, he sank to his knees, leaning against the wall. He thought he heard cries coming from within, but the stone walls were so thick that it was probably just his imagination.

When the door swung open a few minutes later, it hit him in the chest and face. He fell over, blubbering into the snow. The murderers came out, conversing in a normal tone of voice. He couldn't understand their words.

He was left alone. His throat ached, and the inside of his face burned terribly. In the emergency after the recital, he hadn't put on his overcoat; now his shirt and trousers were soaked through with snow. His right hand was a bloody mess.

He lay there for at least an hour. What had happened—the camp, the futility of it all—began to fade from his mind. He gathered some snow to numb the pain in his hand, tried to soothe the burning in his eyes by rubbing them with snow-covered fingers. He remembered that as a child he'd hated being left alone in the dark, and would hug his pillow as if it were a stuffed animal, or an imaginary friend. The smell of the clean sheets, his mother's good-night kiss, the sound of the door closing as she left—it all came back to him so vividly. He remembered how he used to go sled-riding, how one day he fell off his sled and tumbled down a hill, coming to a stop only at the bottom, too frozen to feel his bruises. He remembered the neutral, watery taste of the snow.

Suddenly there was a boot a few inches from his face. Looking up, he could make out the wire-rimmed glasses, the sharp nose and chin, the hair brushed back from that face he had come to hate so much. The snow on the ground gave off a white glow that seemed to prolong the twilight, and the roving searchlight lent an intermittent distinctness to the shadowy forms of nearby buildings.

The Kommandant was holding something. He extended it toward him, saying, "Here's your violin. You didn't put it away very carefully, so I took the liberty of covering it with the cloth and closing the case."

Keller sat up, took the instrument without a word and held it against his chest, slowly rocking back and forth. He wondered how he could make him pay. But there was nothing he could do to him, no price he could exact for what had been done. All he could hope for was somehow to understand.

"Why did you do it?" His voice sounded strange to him, disembodied, as if someone else were speaking.

The Kommandant just stared at him.

"I thought you would let them go."

"What made you think such a thing?"

"The experiment had to have some purpose. To atone for all the others."

The Kommandant laughed quietly for a moment. "I'm afraid you've confused me with yourself. You see, I feel no guilt for what is done here. You can't seem to believe that the experiment was conducted out of sheer scientific curiosity."

"Scientific curiosity . . ." Keller repeated, shaking his head.

"What good would it have done to keep them alive? Do you think it's proper procedure to reuse laboratory animals once an experiment is completed? We're not cheap, you know. There's an almost unlimited supply."

He saw himself lunge upward and grab him by the throat. He pushed him down, fell on top of him and knocked his head against the ground. His thumbs found that goddamn Adam's apple, almost as hard as a bone, and pressed into it deeper and deeper. The Kommandant's hands struggled frantically to push Keller's away, and the broken glasses danced on the bridge of his nose as his head thrashed from side to side.

But in reality he sat there immobilized and muttered in a voice half-choked with hate, "You called them human beings before."

"Well, maybe you're right," the Kommandant said lightly, as if he hadn't heard the words Keller had just spoken. "Maybe there was another motive besides curiosity. I don't see any reason not to tell you, now that you're involved more deeply than you ever thought possible."

"I don't know what you mean," Keller whispered.

"You know, you get tired of having power over people— that is, the same old power to kill them, day after day. I'll admit there's a thrill to it at first, but after a while the routine starts to take its toll. The monthly quota becomes something of a burden. You get satiated, bored—especially when they don't resist, when they no longer seem to *feel* what you're doing to them. Of course, there are physical methods of evoking a response. But that's too direct, too crude for my taste. I prefer a subtler approach. If you can find a way to raise their hopes, they'll be at your mercy again. All you have to do is reawaken their nerve endings, and the pain you inflict will really hurt them."

There was a hushed excitement in his voice, and his eyes seemed unusually bright in that eerie half-light.

"But you promised me," Keller said, standing up with great effort. He was shaking from the cold. "You promised you would do everything in your power to save them."

"Do you really expect a man like me to keep his promises?" asked the Kommandant in a low voice. "But in this case I actually did. I said nothing about saving them; I only promised I would do everything in my power to fulfill your wishes."

Keller turned his back to him.

"I have done so."

A chill rushed up Keller's spine. "What in hell is that supposed to mean?"

"It means you wished them dead."

"No." Keller began to walk away from him, very slowly. He had some trouble keeping his balance; it felt like he was swaying from side to side with every step he took.

"Yes," said the Kommandant with greedy satisfaction, following him. "Don't try to run away from the truth."

"I wanted you to let them live."

"So you said this morning, but I saw through it right away. It was clever of you to titillate yourself with the notion that you'd risk your life for a humanitarian gesture. And my life, too, while you were at it. How noble you must have felt! And how free of responsibility as you watched them die."

"I had no part in this," Keller murmured without turning around or stopping.

"You could have left earlier, could have washed your hands of the whole thing. But no, you wanted to stay on to watch the executions and get a thrill."

"No! No, damn you!" He quickened his pace and covered his ears in an attempt to shut out the Kommandant's words.

"You're incapable of walking out of hell, even when the gate is opened for you."

"You would have shot us if we had walked through that gate."

"You can say that to yourself; it's a good excuse. But the fact is, you could have walked out as easily as I could."

"You're lying. You were just playing games with us."

"You'll never know for sure." There was a touch of gloating in his voice, and Keller could feel the Kommandant's eyes drilling through the back of his head.

Could they have gotten out? Was there a way he could have saved Grete, or at least avoided being a witness to her murder?

"Why, you carry hell around inside you, and the violin is your instrument of torture. I know: I've read your diaries."

He froze. How the hell had they gotten their hands on his diaries?

The Gestapo.

Finally he understood: they'd chosen him for this experiment because they knew about everything—not only his disgust with the wounded soldiers and their coarseness. It went way beyond what was in his diaries. They must have known about Ernst, and Marietta, and his fake Jewish credentials—and how he felt about music after he walked out of her life.

There was no limit to what they knew.

"You don't forgive your audience so easily for being a witness to your ordeal."

"I don't know what you're talking about."

"Do I really have to spell it out for you? All right, then. You're not good enough to conquer them with your talent, so you want to kill them. And whom do you hate most of all?"

"You!" Keller yelled, wheeling around to face him.

"Yes, of course." He smiled: the violinist's hatred seemed to give him pleasure. "But from the first moment, I knew you'd never lift a finger against me. No, you were too polite to do that. You were ready to obey orders no matter what you thought. A good pawn, the kind of citizen the Reich needs."

Keller started to walk away from him again. The Kommandant was still following him, but seemed to be moving more slowly than before: his voice grew fainter as the distance between them increased.

"You'd never kill anybody—not all by yourself. Oh, no, you're too pure for that. And the morality you cling to is much too precious. So you leave the killing to us."

"And what about you?" Keller called back to him.

"Me? I swim with the current. I don't try to justify my behavior, or excuse it by saying I'm just following orders. You consider me a monster, but how different are we from each other?"

Keller was forced to piece together the fragments of speech that came to him between the howls of the wind.

"The only real difference is, I don't hide from what I am."

"Then why did *you* leave the killing to the guards?" Keller shot back. "You weren't even there."

There was no immediate response to this. Looking back as he walked, the violinist could hardly see him because the snow was falling so thick and fast. But near the main gate he thought he heard these words: "You know, I could have you killed. They say you tried to interfere."

One last time he stopped to listen.

"But I'll let you go. You really present no threat to the Third Reich. In your heart . . . you're an accomplice."

The last words were almost inaudible; it took him a few moments to sort out their meaning. Though the Kommandant's voice was so distant and faint, it seemed as if he had been standing next to Keller, whispering—or as if the end of the sentence had welled up from the depths of his own soul.

XIV

Accomplice. He staggered forward under the weight of that word. The guards opened the gate and he passed through, wondering if the trap he had avoided the night before would close on him now. The Kommandant hadn't offered any guarantee of his safety; there was no way to be sure they weren't lifting their guns to their shoulders and taking aim that very moment, waiting until he was just at the limit of their range. Letting him build up hope: by now he knew how much they enjoyed that sort of game.

Keller didn't look back, trying to get away from the lights of the camp as quickly as he could without running. When he reached the end of the short road that led away from the gate, he came to the rail loading platform and turned right. He wasn't sure of the way home, but decided that if he followed the tracks, at least he would be starting out in the right direction.

There had been a full moon the night before; the sky had been radiant with stars that would have lit his way home had he ventured through the open gate. Tonight, though, he was afraid he'd lose his way in the dark, but the whiteness of the snow on the ground and in the air seemed to reflect some moonlight. He decided to avoid the main road, walking parallel to it on the other side of the tracks. Even the road, which must have been plowed that day—he'd seen Wehrmacht trucks moving on it as he walked to the "concert hall" for his final performance—was already blanketed with snow. At the edge of the field where he was trudging along, the drifts were so deep that he sank up to his calves with every step, and stumbled again and again.

After fifteen minutes he came to a fork in the road, which he didn't remember from the day he was driven to the camp. He thought of the warehouse full of stolen shoes, the inmates hauling sacks and crates onto the train: the rail line must lead to Frankfurt or Berlin, or some major depot, not to a small town like his. So he chose the fork that led away from the tracks, still careful to walk near the road but not on it, so as to avoid any vehicles that might be moving toward or away from the camp.

He didn't dare think about the next day or beyond. He was heading home, but could no longer imagine himself living there. How could he get out of bed every morning and look at himself in the mirror? How could he ever bear to pick up the violin and practice? He kept picturing the hollow, staring eyes, the poor bodies shaking, turning blue in the wind. And that pile of rotting corpses in the pit. He was feverish already, on the verge of getting the chills, but it was rage that shook him and dogged his footsteps.

Rage and shame: he remembered Grete breaking down after she told him how her family had been wiped out, could still feel her tears soaking his collar. He recalled the serenity with which she faced her tormentors moments before she died, and he knew that those guards—and he himself—would never be capable of such dignity in the face of death.

Walking had become such a struggle that he finally made up his mind to get back onto the road after all, because he'd never make it home like this. But by now the snow was falling so fast, the wind driving it into his eyes with such fury, that he couldn't find the pavement. He'd lost his bearings, could no longer tell if his steps, as he gritted his teeth and pulled his legs up, were carrying him forward, sideways, or even back toward the camp.

Having fallen for the hundredth time, he couldn't find the strength or will to pick himself up again. The wind seemed to have died down somewhat, at least for the moment. He lay there a few minutes, looking at a row of trees not far away, wondering if there might be a house nestled among them, or a barn in one of those fields, or a hut—any place where he could seek some shelter.

Soon the wind shifted, blowing snow in his face once again. He bowed his head, then felt a layer of moist flakes gathering on his hair, nose and eyelashes. Burying his face in his hands, he realized that this was the only shelter he could find right now—to stay down, not to get up and struggle against the wind. He would wait until he'd regained some strength, until the snow stopped coming down.

Why do I have to get home tonight at all?

It would be easier to find his way in the daylight, he reasoned. He relaxed his grip on the handle of his violin case, yielding to a sense of relief.

He knew what happened to people who fell asleep in a snowstorm. But he was so exhausted that he no longer cared. And in his growing numbness he began to ask himself why he should live when they had died.

It occurred to him that his violin, which he'd always protected as if it were his child, would be buried along with him, that a great instrument would be lost forever because he had used it in a perverted experiment. He tried to picture the warm red glow of its varnish and the gorgeous flames radiating outward from the seam that ran down the two-piece back. But here everything was cold and grayish-white. There was no color left in his world, nothing but layer upon layer of white on the ground, driving, swirling lines of white in the air, gray streaks against the surrounding darkness. He looked at the case, already half submerged, yearning for the warmth of those colors. His fingers were already fumbling at the lock when he changed his mind: whatever might happen to the violin after he perished, he was not going to open that case in a blizzard and ruin a Guarnerius simply in order to gaze at it one last time.

He closed his eyes. The deepening hush of the snowfall was punctuated only by the shrieks of occasional wind gusts. Fragments of music began to pass through his head, motivic shards that gradually took on the pulse of a slow triple meter and coalesced into shadows of recognizable patterns. What was this music, so infinitely quiet, filtering into his mind from so far away? The near-frozen fingers of his left hand aligned themselves with the continuous flow of melody, pressing gently against the top of his violin case in imaginary chords and double-stops. It was the *Chaconne!*—so pure, so beautiful, and now so . . . untouchable. It was just a few hours ago that he had played it, before his world had irreparably darkened. He lay there and listened to the magisterial unfolding of the sublime variations in D major, felt himself pulled gently upward, as if he was floating along the giant arc of their ascent from tranquil reflection to fervent affirmation and then rapture.

But there was an abrupt shift, the resignation of the return to D minor, which now spelled desolation: he knew he'd never play this music again. He couldn't bear to hear it any longer, couldn't face what was coming in a few lines—that pedal tone on the open A string, the other voice descending stepwise, becoming chromatic but always drawn back into the resonance of that A, a distant knell gathering strength, drawing nearer.

It took a spasm of will to pull himself out of his reverie. He had to concentrate on the here and now, not on the music of a world that no longer existed. He couldn't stay there all night; he'd never survive. He'd get up in a few minutes. Just a few more minutes to rest, he told himself. It didn't matter that he might not make it anyway, or that he had nothing left to look forward to. He had to try. He owed it—to *them*. The war would be over soon, and someone would have to bear witness.

The first thing he had to do was avoid being mesmerized by those final variations, by that bell tolling from afar.

But he found, as had often happened in the past, that it was not so easy to dislodge a piece of music from his mind, and if he wanted to stop it from going forward, it would simply double back on itself, on the part he had already heard, in an endless loop. The only way to get rid of it was to yield to a substitute obsession—another tune.

"Gebt mir meinen Jesum wieder" sprang into service, its bouncy, rollicking theme and showy little scales and arpeggios forming an absurd contrast to the solemnity of the Chaconne and the desolation that surrounded him, to the wet and cold that were seeping into his bones. The last thing he wanted to think about now was the clink of those silver pieces on the Temple floor, and the hand that had thrown them.

My God, do I have to die with this cheerful tune running through my mind?

He tore at his hair, pounded his forehead with the flat of both hands in an attempt to achieve silence.

———————

A low rumble. Continuous, getting louder. Was it the noise in his head, the hiss that plagued him at night and robbed him of sleep, worse than usual because this barren snowscape had sucked away all the normal sounds of the world? Was this the only silence he could aspire to?

But no, it wasn't in his head.

He looked up. Aircraft? Finally coming to bomb that God-forsaken camp? He couldn't see more than a few feet up, and besides, the noise was coming from his right. It was the rumble of a car engine. Two beams of light projected onto the field not far from where he lay; he hadn't strayed far from the road after all. With his last ounce of strength he staggered to his feet and pulled the violin up from its bed of snow, not knowing whether he should move toward or away from the car. Had they come to save him, or . . .

"Get in!" The thin, reedy voice was raised, but not in a tone of command. Not a bark. "Come on, get in," he heard as he moved a few steps closer. It sounded as if there was a note of pleading in the repetition, not impatience. Finally, beyond the glare of the headlights, through the haze of white, he could make out the driver's face. It was Rudi at the wheel, half turned toward him, his lips slightly parted, his brow creased.

"You . . . you came by yourself." Gottfried was surprised by the sound of relief in his own voice.

Rudi nodded.

"He sent you to finish the job?"

"No."

"To get rid of an inconvenience. Close the books on an experiment."

"You're wrong. He could have let you flounder around and freeze to death. And if he'd wanted to be sure and get rid of you, he would have sent someone else."

Gottfried took a few more steps toward the car, almost believing him. As he grabbed the door handle, though, it struck him that the Kommandant might have sent Rudi on this mission as a final test of loyalty. After all, it would be much harder for him to kill a musician he admired than to kill a nameless Jew. But his colleagues would have had no trouble with it.

"For Christ's sake, what are you waiting for? I've come to take you home."

He saw no weapon in the car, and the urge to collapse into the back seat was too strong to resist.

———————

Rudi shifted gears and the car began to move. For a few minutes neither of them spoke. Gottfried remembered the first time they'd met, barely two days before, and the surprise he had felt to discover a fellow music-lover in that camp. He could only recall the earnestness of their debate about the *St. Matthew Passion* as if it had taken place on the other side of a great divide, in an earlier epoch of his life, an age of innocence. True, he had already figured out that terrible things were happening in the camp, but he was unaware of Rudi's role in them. And his own hands had still felt clean.

Irretrievable. The past.

"I was in the back of the room. You didn't see me, did you?"

"When?"

"Today, while you were playing the Bach. I had slipped in

just before you started—while you were tuning your violin—
and you didn't notice I was there. I didn't want the Jews to
see me either, but they never seemed to notice much, anyway."

"Why did you come?"

"It was your last performance at the camp. I thought you
might play the Chaconne—maybe because we had talked
about it—and I didn't want to miss that. I wasn't sure I'd ever
get to hear it again."

"Well, I hope it was worthwhile," Gottfried muttered.

"It was so beautiful. I was sitting on the floor, in the corner, with tears dripping down my cheeks."

"Oh, come on! You expect me to believe that, when you
were about to shoot a man in the head?"

Rudi turned and looked at him for a moment, long
enough for Gottfried to see the hurt in his face. The car
swerved, but he turned around in time to correct his steering.
Gottfried heard him sigh. When he finally spoke, his voice was
drained of energy, colorless.

"You don't have to believe it if you don't want to, but it's
true."

"I suppose you were already mourning the Jews you and
your friends were about to kill."

"It wasn't the Jews I was crying for. And the others—
they're not my friends. No, I don't claim to be able to cry for
the Jews anymore. You can think I'm a monster if that makes
you feel any better."

His words echoed the Kommandant's, both implying that
beneath the surface, Gottfried was like them.

"I don't think you're a monster," he said wearily. What was
the use of trying to hold Rudi accountable? He found himself
beginning to soften, to feel sorry for him.

But why should he feel any sympathy for Rudi when it was the Jews who had died?

"I just don't want to hear any sentimental lies. Not after what happened today."

"Don't worry, I'll tell you the truth. No whitewash, no excuses. I don't pretend to be what you'd call a civilized person anymore, even if I do love music. I've been at the camp too long. About the Jews: I know it's not their fault, but I'm tired of reminding myself that they're human beings. At first I was horrified at the way they were treated, but now I'm used to it. All I can feel now is disgust. Disgust at the way they look and smell, even the way they move."

"So who were you crying for? Yourself? Your lost innocence?"

"The music was so beautiful. I . . . I'd never heard anything like it, not from a single violin. The recording I told you about was nothing compared to it. I had the feeling you'd never played like that before, that you were stretching beyond yourself, way beyond what anyone could do in a normal concert. I didn't want it to end. I could have stayed in that corner forever."

All his life, Gottfried had hoped and waited for praise like this, and now it meant nothing to him. He couldn't even muster the energy to respond graciously. Rudi's rhapsodizing was an irritant, not a comfort.

His throat felt parched; he would have given anything for a glass of water. He gathered some snow in his hands and brought them to his mouth, trying to suck in some moisture.

"You know, my gun was lying on the floor beside me. It never looked so strange to me as when I listened to you play. So . . . alien. I never wanted to touch that gun again. I wanted time to stop. But when you came to the part that sounds like a bell tolling—you know, when you keep playing the same note, with other notes moving against it, and the whole thing gets louder and louder—I knew it would be over soon."

"You mean you knew what was going to happen."

"Yes," he admitted in a low voice.

"You could have told me. This morning, or yesterday."

"What good would that have done? It wouldn't have changed anything."

"Yes. It might have. I don't think I could have played like that if I'd known for sure there was no hope. I might have gone through the motions, but he wouldn't have got what he wanted."

"They'd still be dead. And then we wouldn't have shared such . . . such beauty."

" 'We'? No, Rudi, don't include yourself. You didn't share a musical experience with the Jews. They disgusted you, remember? And what the hell good did the music do them?"

"Listen, they had to die. There was no hope for them, you just didn't know that. Well . . . if you have to die, it must be better to have Bach ringing in your ears."

"That's a bit too lofty for me right now. Maybe it's worse."

"You haven't been there, watching them for months. You don't know the level they were reduced to—what animals they had become. No, hear me out. Day after day I've watched them die. And I've watched them live, too—if you can call that living."

"You haven't only watched."

"Yes, that's true. Sometimes I've been forced to kill them. But you can't feel sorry for each and every one." He flicked some snow off his coat. "They're better off dead, anyway."

"You have no right to say that."

"What's right got to do with it?" He snorted. "You haven't

been there. What a luxury: you can still consider yourself a human being, with normal human responses. But I have no compassion left. That's a luxury I can't afford, not if I want to survive. The only thing I can cling to is music. It's the only thing that makes me feel remotely human in the midst of all that." He lifted one hand from the wheel in an oblique gesture back toward the camp, then let it fall onto the seat beside him. "That's what you gave us today. For a few moments you made us human again."

"*They* were always human."

They drove on in silence. Gottfried could sense the motion of the car, but there were no landmarks against which to measure any forward progress: it seemed as if they were riding on a giant treadmill, covering the same ground in the same torrent of snow from one moment to the next. He didn't understand how Rudi could see enough to keep the car on the road; the headlights illuminated only a kaleidoscope of swirling snowflakes. Gottfried closed his eyes to avoid getting dizzy from the chaotic, ever-shifting lines of white etched against the darkness.

When Rudi spoke again, he had to raise his voice to be heard against the wind. "You want to know why I was crying? I know you think it's sentimental, disgusting—a killer who cries. You think my tears defiled the music. But I wasn't feeling sorry for myself. I wasn't mourning my lost innocence, or my childhood, or my days at the university in Leipzig before everything fell apart. No. I was mourning the music itself, *our* music, the music that can never be the same again. Not after the ovens. Not after the burial pit. Not after we've distorted music by blasting it through our loudspeakers while we count them and herd them like cattle. I used to think it didn't matter what they did to waltzes and tangos, that our great music would survive all this, that it would remain pure. How stupid I was! They've ruined everything, they've pulled it down to their level, dragged the summits of our culture through a cesspool."

"And I've helped them."

Once again Rudi was silent. He hunched his shoulders, shook his head as he steered through the blizzard. Somehow Gottfried sensed that Rudi wanted to back away from the edge of the abyss he had just described. As for him, his arms and legs and neck had begun to ache. He had nothing more to say to Rudi; all he wanted was to lie back and be quiet. And get home to his bed.

"If I ever get out of this nightmare alive, I hope to be able to go to a concert again someday. Years from now, if you're playing somewhere, I'd like to come backstage and . . ." His voice trailed off. He must have known he was dreaming—there would be no such concert.

"I will never play again," Gottfried murmured. He wasn't sure Rudi had heard him: he barely had the strength to speak. His clothes were hanging on him like a wet sack, and he had the chills.

"Maybe it will have to be different music from now on. I can understand . . . some memories take a long time to shake off." Competing with the wind, Rudi's voice had risen to a hopeless whine.

"I will never play the violin again!" Gottfried shouted.

The car went into a skid. Rudi stepped on the brakes. Instinctively Gottfried's left hand shot out toward the violin as he braced himself with the right. They spun around in a wide, bumpy arc before lurching to a stop. Rudi leaned over the steering wheel and spread his fingers out on the dashboard, the knuckles arched. His shoulders were heaving.

"Can't you forgive me?" There was a catch in his voice.

"How can I forgive you when I can't forgive myself?" Gottfried's voice was shaking, too, but for a different reason. His teeth had begun to chatter. Rudi turned around, his face wet with snow and tears. He put his hand on Gottfried's forehead.

"My God," he gasped. "You're burning up."

"I'm freezing," Gottfried muttered.

"Here, take this." Rudi pulled off his coat and handed it to him. "Cover yourself with it." Gottfried was too weak to resist the offer.

Rudi turned back to the wheel and started driving again, more carefully now but as fast as he safely could. Gottfried no longer tried to speak, and Rudi seemed to know better than to tax him with more pleas for understanding or forgiveness. Gottfried lay down and dozed off. When he opened his eyes, they were winding through the dimly lit, familiar streets of his town. Within a few minutes they pulled up in front of his building. It seemed like much longer than half a week since he had last seen it. Rudi helped him up the four flights to his garret, and he collapsed into bed without even taking off his clothes.

"You should change into something dry."

"I will in a few minutes, once you leave."

"Let me get you some aspirin."

"It's in the cupboard, over the sink."

Rudi poured some water into a glass and brought it over to the bed, helping Gottfried prop himself up just enough to swallow the aspirin.

"I have to get you a doctor."

"The only doctor in this town died of a heart attack last month. Please, just let me rest."

"I'll let the Wehrmacht know you're sick. They must have a doctor somewhere in the area."

"They're all near the front. I just need to rest. Please, leave me in peace."

"Yes, I suppose I should go. It's time for me to get back to the camp now—the Kommandant will be wondering." He moved toward the door. "But we'll have the Wehrmacht send someone to look in on you in the morning. We borrowed you, and we ought to return you in decent shape."

"Rudi," called Gottfried in a voice so weak it sounded like a whisper.

His hand on the knob, Rudi turned and looked at him one last time.

"You saved my life out there. I just wanted to say thank you."

"There's no need," he said, squinting slightly and running one hand through his hair. "No . . . human being would have let you freeze to death."

He pulled open the door. "I hope," he added softly, looking out toward the stairwell, "that after this is all over . . ." He hesitated, clearing his throat.

"I don't know what to hope anymore." Incapable of offering comfort, Gottfried looked at the forlorn figure in the doorway and said, "Goodbye, Rudi," then gathered the down quilt between his knees, shifted onto his side and closed his eyes. A few moments later he heard the door shut, and the first few halting steps down the stairs.

Threadsuns

over the gray-black wasteness.
A tree-
high thought
strikes the light-tone: there are
still songs to sing beyond
humankind.

—Paul Celan

Author's Note

The events in this novel that take place between 1933 and '35 are based on the life of my father, the violinist Ernst Drucker, who graduated from the Hochschule in Cologne in 1933 and eventually became concertmaster of the Jewish Kulturbund Orchestra in Frankfurt and later in Berlin. He emigrated to the United States with the rest of his family in September 1938.

A year after my father's death in 1993, I read the autobiography of Albert Speer, and was surprised to learn that Siegfried Borries, one of my father's acquaintances from his days at the Hochschule, had flown to Finland with Speer late in the war. After Speer and other top officials from the war ministry had inspected the fortifications on the front line between the German troops, their Finnish allies and the Russian enemy, they built a campfire and listened to Borries perform Bach's Chaconne under the stars. I regret having missed the opportunity to ask my father what he knew about Borries's prejudices and political affiliations in the early 1930s.

One day in the spring of 1933, my father found his name stricken from the program of the upcoming graduation concert at the Hochschule. It was his teacher Bram Eldering—also the teacher of the world-famous Adolf Busch, in whose quartet my father later played—who threatened to resign if his pupil was not allowed to play at least the first movement of the Brahms Concerto. It was my father who wrote a letter to the editor of the *Völkischer Beobachter,* in response to a perfunctory and racist review, pointing out that Brahms had dedicated his "immortal German violin concerto" to Joseph Joachim, a Jew.

Some of the bizarre moments in Keller's performances for the wounded soldiers are loosely based on my own experiences performing in hospitals, an alcoholics' ward, a drug rehabilitation center and a psychiatric ward while preparing for the Queen Elisabeth International Violin Competition in Brussels in 1976.

Acknowledgments

For their encouragement and guidance during the long, intermittent gestation of this book, I am grateful to Thomas Gavin, Denise Levertov, Eileen Lottman, Richard Pollak, Jef Geeraerts, J. B. Keller, John Felstiner, Carlotta Maurice, Stephen Donadio and Martha Cooley. Special thanks are due Elizabeth Benedict, who patiently read three successive versions of the story and offered many valuable insights.

A nearly final version eventually found its way to Simon & Schuster through the generosity and interest of Kate Atkinson, Peter Straus and my wonderful agent, Melanie Jackson. I am indebted to David Rosenthal and all his colleagues at Simon & Schuster who have been involved with this novel, particularly to my editor, Sarah Hochman, who from the beginning of our work together demonstrated a clear and deep grasp of what I was trying to achieve.